SANCTIONS
IN *Paradise*

SANCTIONS IN *Paradise*

PETER NICHOLL

To order additional copies of this book, contact:
Xlibris
NZ TFN: 0800 008 756 (Toll Free inside the NZ)
NZ Local: 9-801 1905 (+64 9801 1905 from outside New Zealand)
www.Xlibris.co.nz
Orders@Xlibris.co.nz
852784

CONTENTS

Chapter One

THE FIRST SHOT

The view from the High Commissioner's extensive lawn was spectacular. All the guidebooks I had read before coming to Seychelles had emphasised that the Seychelles had the only granitic ocean islands in the world. I had not realised the significance of that until I came. There were thirty-two granite islands and around seventy to eighty coralline islands, some of which were little more than a patch of sand and a few trees. The granite islands accounted for most of the country's land area and were much more rugged and mountainous than other tropical islands.

The capital, Victoria, was laid out below the High Commissioner's lawn and was backed by huge granite rock faces, one of which was over a thousand feet high and sheer. The topography was quite different to that of the South Pacific islands I had visited. The vegetation was similar, to my inexpert eye at least. It was the luxurious and all-enveloping vegetation that was the dominant impression left from my visits to Fiji, Western Samoa and Rarotonga in the Cook Islands. In the Seychelles, however, the massive rock faces made more impact than the vegetation. They made man and man-made structures look insignificant.

The view out to sea was similar to some I had seen in the South Pacific - only better. The sea was calm and multi-hued, the darker shades indicating areas of coral reef. I was looking forward to exploring those reefs. There was a group of islands in the foreground. I had read the guide books carefully and knew that they were St. Anne, Round, Long, Moyenne and Cerf Islands, though I could not remember which was which. The mixture of French and English names was typical of the place names in this bi-cultural society. The set of islands lay to the right of the entrance to Victoria Harbour. In the distance I could see a large island which one of the Seychellois delegation had told me was Praslin, the second largest island in the Group.

Victoria itself was the least spectacular part of the view. It looked insignificant compared with the magnificence of its setting. The setting deserved something more. There were no tall buildings, three stories being the maximum. That I regarded as a plus for tall buildings would have seemed out of place and intrusive in that setting. But few of the buildings had any great charm. Most of them were old – not so old that they had acquired the stature that comes with great age - just old with a. faintly run down air. The newest and grandest-looking building was that of the Central Bank of Seychelles, a three-storey building of marble and glass that reflected the highest granite cliff in its windows. It struck me that wherever they are located, one thing that Central Banks are good at is housing themselves in luxurious buildings. My gaze tended to skip quickly across the city to its harbour, the sea and the offshore islands, all of which gave Victoria a setting to be envied.

Even the scene on the lawn itself was spectacular. The first social event of the Annual Conference of Commonwealth Ministers of Finance was this formal welcome to the visiting delegations by the British High Commissioner to Seychelles. The reception was held at his residence high on a hill overlooking Victoria. The diversity of the Commonwealth 'family', as the Secretary General of the Commonwealth Secretariat, Sonny Ramphal, was in the habit of referring to the forty-nine members of the Commonwealth, was evident from the dress and appearance of the delegates. While business suits were worn by most, some of the African and Asian delegates were wearing their traditional dress and the Fijian and Tongan delegations were both wearing lava-lavas, a skirt-like outfit that was the traditional male dress in their countries. It was an impressive and colourful scene.

My attention was dragged back to the group of people I was standing with. I realised that I had been asked a question and they were awaiting my response. The problem was that because of my daydreaming, I had no idea what the question was. I was in a small group of six of the younger participants in the Conference In the presence of so many 'elder' politicians and bureaucrats, the small number of us that had not yet reached or could still clearly remember thirty had tended to gravitate towards each other. In the group were John Blake, a British journalist covering the Conference for the 'Observer', Simone Lablanche, a member of the Canadian delegation whose job as personal assistant to her Minister of Finance seemed to be similar to mine in New Zealand, Eliphaz Ruheni, one of the officials with the Kenyan delegation, Chris Braithewaite from Trinidad and Tobago and Andrew Mayhew of the British delegation.

I apologised and asked if they could repeat the question. John Blake had asked me if I thought anything other than the issue of whether or not the Commonwealth should apply economic sanctions against South Africa would make progress at this Conference. "I think the Conference will get bogged down on that one issue," I replied. "What do you mean by bogged down?" Ruheni interjected. "Don' t you think that issue is so important that it deserves to completely absorb our attention?"

Lesson number one I thought to myself as I realised how careful one had to be about what one said in order to avoid arousing sensitivities at a meeting like this. I was endeavouring to extricate myself from the verbal quicksand when a sharp, sudden noise interrupted me. The noise was not that loud and seemed to come from some distance away. It could easily have been a car back firing. I, and most of the people around me, only realised it was a gunshot when John Blake gave a gasp, staggered back and fell. The realisation that the noise had been a shot and someone at the reception had been the target spread around the guests - slowly at first and then with increasing speed like ripples in a pool.

Pandemonium soon developed. Most people pushed towards the safety of the house in an undignified scramble that tipped over tables and chairs and sent some of the older and slower moving delegates sprawling., If people were too far away from the residence they took what shelter they could find behind hedges and trees. As there was considerable confusion over the direction that the shot had come from, there was considerable uncertainty over which side of a hedge or tree would provide the most effective shelter. In other circumstances some of the scenes of confusion would have been amusing. Eliphaz Ruheni, showing coolness in the midst of the general panic, hurriedly ushered Simone Lablache into the house as soon as he realised what had happened.

Without really thinking, I knelt down to see if I could help John Blake. One of the Seychellois waiters also came to see if he could help. I had no knowledge of first aid, a weakness I had vowed to overcome many times but never got around to, and I had never previously seen a bullet wound. But it was clear to me that Blake was seriously, probably critically hurt. The wound was in his chest and blood was rapidly turning his white shirt red. As I knelt beside him he clutched my shirt with an intense grip and tried to speak. His voice was weak and indistinct. He seemed to me to say something like 'niss' and then after a delay while he tried to recover some strength, he said something that sounded like 'grey thing'. I looked at the waiter but he shrugged his shoulders in a way that indicated he didn't know what Blake had said. I held Blake's head as carefully as I could and in a voice as calm as I could make it asked, "Could you say that again John?" It was too late. He gave a shudder and collapsed. He had in fact died, though I did not recognise that at the time, never having seen death at close hand before.

No more shots were heard and the scene gradually began to gain some semblance of order. The police and soldiers had taken up positions around the perimeter of the garden and were slowly ushering those guests who had taken shelter outside into the house. Everybody was still very nervous and watchful. A policeman crawled over to our small group, briefly examined Blake and said to me, "There is nothing more you can do for him, Sir, come inside the house." I let him assist me to the house.

Soldiers were scattering into the hills in the general direction it was thought the shot had come from but I felt it was almost certain that they would be too late to find anyone or anything. The hills so dominated the landscape that a person with a powerful rifle and a good scope could have fired the shot that killed Blake from any number of places. The land was so hilly that they had no hope of quickly cordoning areas off. Foot tracks criss-crossed the area providing a myriad of escape routes.

Later that afternoon I had to go to the security room at the Fisherman Cove Hotel, the venue where the Conference was being held.

The reception had been called off early after the High Commissioner had announced that a British journalist had been shot and killed. All delegates had been asked to return to the Fisherman's Cove Hotel and remain within the hotel for the rest of the day. There had been some who had argued with that directive - it denied them the opportunity to sample Seychelles' night-life and for some the opportunity to let their hair down away from their home cities was the main attraction of an international conference. But most had accepted it as a sensible precaution.

There were four men in the office when I went in. Three appeared to be Seychellois, though that was a risky assumption on my part for the Seychellois were an amazing mixture of colours and facial characteristics. The basic mixture was African and European. In some of them Chinese, Indian or Arabic had been thrown in for added variety, so that it was impossible to describe in simple terms the average Seychellois. The other man was European and somehow seemed to hold himself separate from the others. The man behind the desk stood up and held out his hand to be shaken. He looked about thirty: tall, slim and brown-skinned; fine-featured and quite handsome. He did not look like a policeman to me. 'I'm Inspector Hoareau' he said, 'Bernard Hoareau. This is my colleague Phillipe Auguste', he added, indicating a dark-skinned, thick-set man sitting on the left of the desk who nodded his head in my direction but did not hold out his hand. 'And this is Mr. Llewelleyn' indicating the European with a vague wave of his hand. Neither he nor Llewellyn explained who Llewellyn was or his reason for being there and I did not feel inclined to ask. I later found out that he was the senior British Intelligence agent covering security at the Conference. The fourth person was not introduced. He was clearly just the note-taker, but I nodded my head in his direction anyway. I got no response, so I turned my attention back to Inspector Hoareau who had started to talk again.

"Mr White," he said, "we appreciate that you have been through a frightening experience but I'm sure you understand that we need to find out if you have any information that may help us. I nodded.

"There may be something you saw or heard that is significant, even though it may not seem. so to you. So please try and tell us as much detail as you can." I nodded.

"First what did you see at the time the shot went off?" Hoareau asked.

"I was talking to Eliphaz Ruhani of Kenya and was not looking in Blake's direction. He was beside me. I had no idea where the shot came from. I didn't even realise it was a shot until I saw John Blake fall," I replied.

"What did you do after he fell?" Hoareau asked.

"I knelt down to see what had happened to Blake and to see if I could help him in any way. I did not realise how seriously he was hurt until I got down close to him", I said.

"Was he already dead when you got to him?" asked Hoareau. "No", I replied. "When I first knelt down he was still alive and he clutched my shirt and tried to speak. I saw their interest quicken.

"Did he manage to say anything?" the Inspector asked with some sign of hope in his voice.

"He was gasping and his words were difficult to hear," I replied. I was conscious of Hoareau's disappointment. Llewellyn had seemed unmoved by any of it so far.

"But he did manage to get out a few words," I went on, realising as I did so that 'a few words' was an exaggeration. There had only been two words, or three at the most, that I had heard or thought I had heard, and I did not know what any of them meant.

"He said 'niss', whatever that means, and then something that sounded like 'grey thing', though with his accent 1 may have misunderstood," I said.

"Is that all?" asked Hoareau. I nodded.

"What do you think they mean?" he asked.

"I have no idea what they mean," I admitted. I had noticed that there had been an exchange of glances between Hoareau and Llewellyn when I had the first word. I had the feeling that it meant something to them. I was not sure I wanted to know what it was. Generally, I am intensely curious about events going on around me but for once I thought that ignorance may be a safer state.

"Are you quite sure that the second thing Blake said was 'grey thing', "Llewellyn asked. He had for the first time begun to show a modest degree of interest in what was going on since I had mentioned the words. "No, I am not sure at all. That's what it sounded like to me, but it was very indistinct. I asked him to repeat it but it was too late', I responded.

"What else could it have been?" Llewellyn asked tersely. "I don't know. It could have been anything that sounded similar," I said.

"That's no use to us. It could be very important. Make an effort for God's sake," Llewellyn responded even more tersely. By Christ, you're a rude bastard, I thought. I stared at him with what I hoped was scorn but he stared and glared right back. It was me who lowered my eyes. Hoareau tried to smooth things over.

"At the time it happened, did any other possibilities for what it could have been run through your mind?" he asked.

I felt much more comfortable talking to him. Llewellyn succeeded in making me feel that I was on trial. Itried to think back to the moment when Blake had still been alive and I had been holding him.

"I first thought he had said grating, but then I thought it was probably two words as there was a definite pause between the two parts. That's when I thought it was probably 'grey thing'. But I guess the pause may have been due to his condition. So it need not mean it was two words at all. The first part was most distinct and I am fairly certain that was grey. The second bit faded away. I am less sure about it.

I realised that I was rambling on and that I did not know any more than I had already told them. There did not seem to be any point in guessing what it could have been so I stopped talking. I had allowed Llewellyn to unsettle me.

"Did anything else happen that you think could assist us?" Hoareau asked. I could not think of anything.

Hoareau thanked me for my actions at the scene and for my cooperation with their questioniong. Llewellyn said nothing more. I nodded and left. As I closed the door I overheard Llewellyn remark that "he was a useless bastard." It was clear that he was referring to me.

I thought I had better track down my Minister and see if there was anything he wanted me to do. I hoped that would take my mind off the way it was running over and over my first close encounter with death. It seemed amazing to me that I could have been so close to the victim and yet seen and heard nothing useful. I had the uneasy feeling that I had somehow failed; that I should have seen more; that I should \have listened harder. It was clear that Llewellyn was of that view. But my background had not prepared me for a situation like this.. _

I was personal assistant to the New Zealand Minister of Finance, Brian Franklyn. I was a career Treasury officer; thirty-four years of age; unmarried. I had been in the New Zealand Treasury for ten years following the completion of a Master's degree in economics at Canterbury University in the South Island city of Christchurch. I had spent a year on exchange at the Australian Treasury in Canberra three years previously. The rest of my career up until a year ago had been spent in the Treasury's Head Office in Wellington. I had been seconded to the Minister's office over the objections of two or three people on the rank above me at the Treasury, including John Kershaw, one of the other members of our delegation to this Conference. They had all been keen to fill the position themselves because of the close exposure it gave an officer to their Ministerial boss. Through a combination of chance, hard work and a facility for and an enjoyment of writing, I had become the Minister's chief speech writer.

This was the first time the Minister had decided to take me with him on an overseas trip. Usually one of the more senior advisory officers from his office and his press secretary went with him but this time he had decided he needed his speech writer on hand as his speech could not be finalised until the last minute. Those who as a consequence had to stay behind in Wellington in mid-winter while I went off to the tropics had been less than pleased. But as I left the questioning session I had been through with Hoareau and Llewellyn I was feeling far from delighted.

The Minister had been in his room when I phoned and he asked me to come straight over. I briefly gave him the details of my police interview but there was not really much I could tell him and I could tell that he was not very interested. Brian Franklyn had been in politics for a long time, even though he was only ten years older than I was. He had a bachelor's degree in economics and accountancy which was unusual amongst our past Ministers of Finance. Most of them were what one could call enthusiastic amateurs when it came to economics and others did not even warrant that description.

He had been an avid reader and writer on economic issues for all of the fifteen years he had been a member of Parliament. That is also fairly unusual amongst our past Ministers of Finance. He was more impressive as a writer than a speaker, which can be a drawback for a politician. The spoken word has an immediate impact and is then forgotten, except for the overall impression of the politician that its delivery created the written word generally has less immediate impact but because it is permanent, it can be reexamined years later by political opponents, journalists, lobbyists or anyone out to score a point at the writer's expense. At some time or another_, Brian Franklyn had put in writing a view on most economic policy issues and a number of social issues as well. Fortunately for him, his views had been more consistent than most other politicians I had known, both as a set of ideas and in his adherence to them over time. But even he was sometimes embarrassed by what he had written in the past.

He does not enjoy conferences normally but I could tell that he was quite excited about the prospects for the next few days. My position as his personal assistant had meant that I had been close to him for the last year and I felt that I could read his moods fairly accurately. That was not really a major accomplishment as he tended to show his moods quite openly, another drawback for a politician. When he was bored by an issue or a person he found it hard to disguise his feelings and simulate interest. When he was interested in an issue, his interest was a very tangible thing. We ran over his programme for the following day, Sunday. He was to have an informal meeting with the Ministers of Finance from Ghana, the Gambia, Sierra Leone and Nigeria at ten at their request. The topic they would want to discuss was obvious. Then he was to have a working lunch with his Canadian and Australian counterparts. Each of them was meeting with other African and Caribbean Ministers during the morning. They would then meet over lunch to compare impressions and see if there was any common ground in the positions they were prepared to take on the economic sanctions issue. The senior officials in our delegation, the Secretary of the Treasury, Graham Sharp, and the Deputy-Governor of the Reserve Bank, Trevor Barnes, were to attend the lunch, but not the meetings with the developing-country Ministers. The two junior members of the delegations, John Kershaw, Assistant Secretary at the Treasury and myself, were not required at either session. I would be free until the afternoon.

Brian Franklyn wanted me to meet him in his room at 3.00pm on Sunday to discuss what had transpired at the m6rning and lunch-time meetings and try and complete the drafting his speech for the Conference. I had written most of his speech before we left Wellington, using ideas I had got from him and from some of the senior officials who were to be in the Conference delegation, particularly Trevor Barnes_, who was always full of ideas. I had taken advantage of the writer's prerogative to put in one or two ideas of my own as well. The Minister had gone over my draft on the plane. There had been plenty of time for him to qo so as we had had to fly from New Zealand to Hong Kong first in order to catch a flight to Seychelles. The total flying time for us had been around twenty-four hours. He had made two or three changes of substance and removed a couple of my more emotive adjectives that he regarded as 'too much'. He had an abhorence of adjectives in his speeches or articles: he believed facts or statements should explain themselves clearly and unemotionally. Adjectives were almost always aimed at the emotions and were therefore in his mind unnecessary and frequently disruptive. He accepted my view, however, that a speech or article devoid of emotion could be a very dull and we had established a working compromise. Still I knew he liked to reinforce his lesson to me whenever possible so I usually deliberately put in one or two extreme words that I knew he would reject. That kept him happy and generally meant that other points that I thought were important retained their place in the speech.

Chapter Two

FLIGHTS AND FANCIES

We were all under security orders to remain in the hotel precincts for that Saturday night. The younger delegates again gravitated into a group in the bar before dinner and most of us had dined together, though some felt an obligation to join their delegations. I explained that as I had no official duties the following day until 3p.m., I was going to be a tourist for the morning and early afternoon - provided the security restriction was relaxed and we were allowed out of the hotel. I didn't think they could keep over two-hundred delegates cooped up in the hotel for very long. Simone Lablache said that she was in a similar situation so I asked her if she would like to join me. She accepted. I said that I would arrange for a mini-moke, a kind of small jeep with a canvas roof, no side windows and only rudimentary comforts to be available from nine in the morning. Mini mokes seemed to be what most tourists used for transport in Seychelles. They looked a bit dangerous and uncomfortable to me but when in Rome .... I arranged to meet Simone in the lobby at nine and provided we were not still 'confined to barracks', we were going to explore.the island.

John Kershaw, who after myself was the youngest member of our delegation, hinted that he had nothing arranged for the following day and wouldn't mind exploring Mahe as well. I managed to ignore his hints. Two is company, particularly when the second one is female; three is a crowd, particularly when the third one is a first-rate bore and regards himself as a ladies' man as well. Kershaw and I were not the best of friends. Our work had put us on the opposite side of issues quite often and he had an unfortunate tendency to take disagreement personally. He was too proud to ask me outright if he could join us. I could tell he was fuming at my obtuseness but I successfully kept up the act. Then Andrew Mayhew asked me if we minded if he and a friend joined Simone and I. I saw Kershaw become instantly alert but I continued to ignore him. I was not sure about Mayhew, having only met him earlier that day. He seemed a pleasant enough chap but what I had in mind was a half a day alone with Simone.

"Who is the friend?" I asked him. If it was another male, as I suspected it was, then he was out. I was not going to compete for Simone's attention with two rivals. He surprised me.

"I have made friends with a local girl," he said somewhat sheepishly, "and I would like her to join us if I may." "Well that was quick work," I said, playing for time while I thought about it. There were sometimes advantages in having another couple along when one was trying to start a relationship, particularly if that couple already had an established relationship and provided a favourable demonstration effect. Mayhew was offended by my riposte. He was rather straight laced, pompous almost.

"It is not like you think. She isn't just a quick pick up," he said, "I came to Seychelles two weeks ago to assist the British High Commission with their arrangements for this Conference. I met Virginia at the High Commissioner's soon after I arrived and we have seen each other quite a lot since then. 'She is a lovely girl, very respectable' he added, colouring as he did so. He was obviously not normally demonstrative.

I decided to let him off the hook and to take a chance. I said they could join us. John Kershaw started to say something but then thought better of it. I knew he would store the slight away in his memory and look for a way to get his own back later.

I dislike having to get well-dressed for breakfast and, besides, I enjoy the luxury of having breakfast delivered to my room. Whenever I travel, I have my breakfast in my room as much as possible. It makes a pleasant contrast to my usual routine when I am at home in Wellington. There, I usually rise at six and cook myself a reasonably substantial breakfast as I can never be sure when or what I will get for lunch, or sometimes even dinner. Working in Parliament can have rather anti-social hours. So at 8.00am on Sunday morning I had breakfast delivered to my room - cereal, scrambled eggs, fresh paw-paw and passion-fruit juice. Delicious: the perfect way to start the day. It also occurred to me that the other advantage of having breakfast in my room on this occasion was that I would avoid bumping into John Kershaw in the dining room. I did not put it past him to have one more attempt to join Simone, Andrew Mayhew and his girlfriend and I on our expedition.

When I went down to the lobby at nine, Simone was waiting. She was in casual clothes - a crossover top that revealed a lot of her shoulders and a hint of her breasts and shorts that revealed a shapely pair of legs. She was surprisingly well-tanned. She looked quite stunning. The weather was fine and the day was already quite hot. I had not heard anything more about security restrictions and I decided not to make enquiries. The instructions yesterday had been to remain in the hotel overnight. I assumed therefore that it no longer applied. We had to wait a few minutes for Mayhew and we left as soon as he arrived. I was anxious to get away before something happened to change our plans for the morning. Nobody stopped us as we walked to the car park or as we drove out of the hotel. The day looked distinctly promising and the events of yesterday slipped out of my mind.

The mini-moke proved to be even more basic than I had expected. Not only were there no side windows, there were no doors as such. One simply climbed in through the gap between the canvas roof and the chassis. But is was cool and it gave a certain sense of adventure. I had a good map, something I always had ever since I tried to drive in England for the first time, managed to miss the Dartmouth Tunnel and ended up lost in the centre of London when I had intended to miss the centre of London altogether. We had to drive into Victoria to pick up Mayhew's girlfriend so we decided to do a circuit of the northern part of Mahe Island before ending up at Beau Vallon Beach. The Conference hotel was on this beach but it was a very long beach and we intended to swim and sunbathe at the other end of the beach, well away from the Conference hotel. Beau Vallon was generally regarded as the best beach on Mahe. There were two other large hotels on the beach, the unoriginally named Beau Vallon Bay Hotel and the Coral Strand Hotel. I was aiming for a spot mid-way between them so that we could have a drink at each of them without having to walk. The circuit we were on took us back over the hills to Victoria and then followed the coastline up the east side of the island, around the northern point and part way back down the west coast. In all, it was a journey of only about thirty kilometres. The roads themselves were surprisingly good but there were a large number of pedestrians and they seemed to be all over the road - at least that is how it felt until I got used to them. On Sunday mornings, most of the Seychellois went to church. They seemed to combine a love of fun and a zest for life with a conscientious attitude to religion and church with a refreshing naturalness. The happy, casual people we passed going off to church seemed such a contrast to the memories of my youth - going to church had been a serious business, not something to enjoy. Laughter and joy had seemed to be the antithesis of religion and church from my experiences, whereas here they mingled easily. Most of the people going to church walked. As there were no footpaths in many of the areas in which we drove, except in Victoria itself, they walked on the road. They had an amazing confidence that vehicles would avoid them. I found it hard to look at the scenery as I had to concentrate on the road and the pedestrians; which was a great pity.

SImone, free of the need to worry about avoiding pedestrians kept up a running commentary on the beautiful or unusual among the sights we passed. Andrew Mayhew, sitting in the back seat, said nothing as we drove over the St Louis Hill. As we neared Victoria I remarked on how quiet he had been and asked him if he was okay.

"Yes, I am fine, thank you Peter. I just hope that you and Simone like Virginia. I think she is one of the nicest people I have ever met. I hope you do too," he replied

I realised that he was worrying about what we would think of his local girlfriend. From what I had seen already there were a lot of beautiful women in Seychelles. They had marvellous skin, most of them dressed very well and walked well. It is hard to explain exactly what I mean by that but if you see a woman who walks well you recognize it instantly. Seychellois women were proud, they certainly weren't shy. One guidebook had described them as French enough to have a good figure; English enough to be well-behaved; Asian enough to possess that hint of the exotic; African enough to harbour the call of the wild.' I had not been in Seychelles long enough to know whether or not the English quality was an accurate description but I had seen enough already to believe the other three were accurate. They were also bold. If one looked at a woman here they did not turn their head or avert their gaze. They looked right back. As you judged them, they judged you.

I could not visualise Andrew Mayhew establishing a relationship with one of these beautiful, direct women of Seychelles. He seemed too straight-laced and pedantic. I was amazed therefore when we eventually got to Virginia's house and Mayhew brought her down to introduce her to us. She was beautiful. She was tall, probably five feet nine or ten. She had smooth, brown skin, medium length dark hair and a fine-textured face that took my breath away. I realised I was staring at her as they walked towards the car and I had to shake myself to resume a more natural expression., She definitely walked well but in a more reserved manner than most Seychellois women. Somehow, she seemed a little less sure of herself as a woman than most of the other Seychellois I had seen. I got out of the car as they approached in order to be able to greet her directly. As Mayhew introduced us, I contemplated switching my attention from Simone to Virginia Renaud but I could tell there was something that went beyond a passing fancy between the two of them. I looked at Mayhew as they spoke to Simone to try and see what Virginia could see in him. He was certainly tall and handsome in a sallow English way but he seemed too dull to attract such a beauty.

Once we got through Victoria and on to the coast road I was able to look around me more as we drove as there were fewer pedestrians. The coastline was right out of the travel brochures - sandy beaches by the score, huge granite boulders, glimpses of the reef, offshore islands. Many of the little bays around the northern point were deserted. It was very tempting to stop and explore them all. Each of the bays was edged by nature-made sculptures of granite and backed by large Takamaka trees that hung out over the sand making inviting, shady and private nooks.

The sand, being corraline, was much whiter than the beach sand in my home country. I am sure everyone has an image in their mind of the perfect tropical island beach. I had such an image and so did Simone.

Here our images were matched by reality around virtually every corner we turned. In contrast to the invariant beauty of the natural scenery, the man-made scenery we passed was quite a mixture. There were a few stunningly impressive houses, including one in solitary splendour on a point jutting out into the sea that had it's own squash court, clearly identified as a 'private court, no entry.' There was another house with high wrought• iron gates with brick surrounds. The gate posts were topped by bronze eagles. I had taken it to be the American Ambassador's residence as a consequence of the eagles but had found out later that it belonged to a Bahreni prince who visited just once or twice a year.

At the other extreme, some of the local housing was little more than shacks and most of them had animals around them - chickens, pigs and the occasional cow. The latter were always tethered but the chickens and pigs roamed at will. Ironically, they seemed to have more road sense than their owners. However, the houses were all neat and tidy.

It was a strong temptation to stop at one of the small coves but we stuck to our plan and carried on to Beau Vallon Bay. We drove slowly and enjoyed the sights, enjoyed the warmth and enjoyed each other's company. In the back of the car, Mayhew and his girlfriend were in a world of their own and Simone and I left them to their mutual admiration. The hotels we passed all looked impressive - the Vista do Mar, the Sunset, the Northolme, the Coral Strand. As we passed each one, Simone and I debated whether we would like to stay in that hotel if we were visiting Seychelles as tourists. We fancied the Vista do Mar because of its views but we concluded that it would not make much difference where one stayed, the sea was no more than a few metres from any of them.

We drove on until we came to the Beau Vallon Bay Hotel in the heart of the beach. We parked the moke in the hotel car-park and walked through the hotel to the beach. The sight when we got there was breath-taking - for a variety of reasons. The beach itself had some of the whitest sand that I had ever seen and it stretched for a kilometre or so in either direction. There were trees right along the top of the beach over its whole length. The .sea was calm and very blue and so clear that one could see the bottom of the sea for a considerable distance out from shore.

Adding to the natural attractions were the human attractions. The beach and the sea were both well-populated, though far from crowded. The people came in all shapes and sizes. A goodly proportion of the female sunbathers were topless. What they were displaying also came in all shapes and sizes. I found it quite fascinating. Simone reacted coldly to my suggestion that she adopt what was obviously the custom for this beach.

We lay on the beach, we swam, we lay on the beach again. We had an early and light lunch at the Coral Strand Hotel. Andrew Mayhew and Virginia joined us for lunch and we found out a bit more about her. Her father was British, her mother Seychellois. Her father, who had been a lot older than her mother, had been a British colonial officer in the days long before independence, which had only come in 1976. He had died many years ago and left them well-provided for. She had two older sisters. Both were married and lived overseas.

One was married to another Seychellois and was living in Melbourne, Australia. The other had married an American who had come to work at the large U.S. sattelite tracking station that was located on one of the peaks of Mahe. She had returned to the States with him at the expiration of his two-year term. Virginia said this was a frequent occurrence.

After lunch Simone and I returned to the beach. During the morning I had watched people being towed around the bay behind a power-boat on a type of parachute. I tried to persuade Simone to have a turn but she said she did not like heights. I was not that keen on heights myself but Simone turned my attempted persuasion of her back on myself and I was too proud to admit tha t the prospect worried me also. I put on a brave front and said I would try it. I had to wait while a Japanese woman had her turn. That took some time. Her husband or boyfriend had to carefully catch each stage of the event on film. There were shots of the run down the beach, the take-off, the flight itself, the landing in the sea,. the swim to the beach and then a breathless description, in Japanese, of the whole thing.

Eventually it was my turn. For some reason Simone seemed to find

the strapping of the harness I had to wear and the instructions I had
to listen to hilarious. She was joined in her laughter by the local beach
boys who seemed to run the paragliding for the hotel. They obviously
had an eye for a pretty woman and were happy to join in her efforts to
embarrass me. I tried to ignore them but that was easier said than done.
I·stepped into a harness that in effect formed a seat and was buckled
around my waist. I was told where to hold on to the two straps below
the parachute during take-off, though I could let them go once I was
aloft if I wished. I was told what to do on take-off, what to do once I
and the parachute hit the water at the end of the flight, how to help
adjust the direction and height of the parachute prior to landing by
pulling on some of the side straps and was told to relax and enjoy it. I
was assured it was all perfectly safe. I wondered how I had got myself
into such a situation.

My instructor then signalled the boatman, who moved the boat off
at speed across the bay. The large pile of rope that lay on the beach in
front of me snaked out rapidly across the sand in a vaguely menacing
fashion. "Go!" shouted the boy and gave me a shove. I ran four or five
paces – I had no choice as the rope was pulling me down the beach
anyway - and suddenly I took to the air as the parachute opened out
behind me. The sensation as I shot into the air with what seemed like
tremendous speed was similar to, but even more dramatic than, that
achieved at the start of a ski run. As I gained height the noise of the
boat disappeared and I imagined that this was as close as man could
get to the sensation of flying. I had never been hang-gliding, it always
seemed like a very high-risk pastime. but I thought that the sensation
was probably similar.

The expression 'a bird's eye view' also took on a real meaning as I
drifted noiselessly some two hundred feet up in the air. The whole of
Beau Vallon Bay and the coastal strip of land behind the bay was laid
out like a carpet below me. Familiar sights, such as our Conference
hotel, took on a different perspective when viewed from high above.
People appeared to be insignificant. I had often had the feeling that
birds treated us earth-bound humans with an air of disdain, almost
one of superiority. Up in the air I felt their attitude was understandable.

The sea was crystal clear and as my flight neared the northern end of Beau Vallon Bay, more and more coral could be seen in its myriad forms. below the surface of the sea. Suddenly, my reverie was broken by something zinging past my head like an angry bee. I didn't know what it was and had just about convinced myself that I had imagined it, when it happened again. I had never been shot at before but the sound I heard was just what I imagined the sound of bullets whistling past one's head would sound like. I yelled to the boat driver to let me down but with the noise of the boat's engine loud in his ears, and the noise of the sea and the breeze also conspiring against me, there was no way I could make him hear me.

I thought of waving my arms and legs about in an effort to attract attention. But I had noticed during the morning that many of the riders on the paraglider had performed amazing acrobatic feats in mid-air so any antics I performed would simply be taken as a sign that I was confident about flying and was enjoying myself. Nevertheless, rather than sit there like a duck in a shooting gallery, I started to sway about as much as I dared while I tried to think of what else I could do. At least I would hopefully distract the aim of the marksman, wherever he was. A third bullet whizzed above me and severed one of the ropes that connected me and my harness to the parachute above. I knew then that it was not my·imagination and I had to make up my mind quickly. The only option I had as far as I could see was to try and lower my height, unbuckle the harness and fall into the sea. I glanced down. Christ, it looked a long way. I had noticed this phenomenon before on diving boards. When one looked at the diving board from the ground it didn't appear to be very high. When one got up on to the board itself the height seemed to have doubled. Two hundred feet viewed from above seemed to be a mile. I pulled on the side straps as hard as I could and the parachute pulled to the left and began to lose some height. The boatman waved his arms to indicate I should stop pulling on the straps. I ignored him and kept pulling until I judged I was down to a safe height. I unbuckled the harness, closed my eyes – and fell.

The shock when I hit the water shot up through my feet and legs, jarred my spine and seemed to lift my head off my shoulders. It was only later that I realised how lucky I was that I hit the water feet first. It had not been deliberate; it just happened to be the way I was aiming when I left the paraglider. But had I hit the water any other way it could have been fatal. Even so my breathe was expelled in a huge gasp of pain as I plunged into the water. It seemed to take forever to struggle back up towards the surface and I was starting to panic when I finally hit the top·again. The boatman circled back and shouted out was I okay. He seemed to be in two minds whether to rescue me or his gear first. I tried to shout 'no, I am not alright', but all that came out was a croak. Still, he realised that I was in some distress. He pulled the boat up near me and with some help from his colleague in the boat, I scrambled in over the side. I lay gasping on the floor of the boat. The boatman asked me, "What the hell you trying to do man, kill yourself?" I was trying to ·save myself from being kille'd. The answer was the exact opposite, but I was too exhausted to answer so he shrugged his shoulders and said something to his mate in Creole, the local patois language, which made them both laugh. They set about hauling their parachute back into the boat. They did not notice the severed chord.

My whole body felt as if it had been stretched on the rack. There was no one area of major pain so I was hopeful that nothing was broken. There were, however, aches in every joint and muscle. So, while one reason for staying on the floor of the boat was safety from the sniper, my body felt incapable of sitting up anyway.

"What happened?" asked the boatman again after he had got his gear back on board and we were heading back towards the beach.

"I was shot at," I whispered. The two Seychellois in the boat looked at each other. The boatman said something to his companion in Creole again and again they both laughed.

I could only surmise what he had said. He probably believed I had an imagination that was too vivid. I was just another one of those crazy tourists. The boatman looked just like Yannick Noah, the French tennis player – dark skin, curly hair and handsome features. His look conveyed scepticism and scorn. I did not have the energy or the inclination t0o try and convince him I was not imagining things so I said nothing more and neither did they.

When we got back near the shore, I asked if they could give me a hand to get to the beach. I was not sure that I could make it on my own and, besides, I felt there may be safety in having other bodies close to mine, though I did not tell them that. They would not have believed me anyway, but if they had, their safety would have been best served by getting as far away from me as possible. 'Yannick Noah' asked his companion to take over the wheel and he leapt into the water and helped me out of the boat.. To my embarrassment, but not my surprise, a large crowd of people had gathered on the beach. I guess it was not every day that someone took a high dive from a paraglider. Simone rushed into the water to assist Yannick Noah. With one of them on either side of me we staggered through the shallows and on to the comforting solidness of the beach. The crowd of curious on-lookers closed around.

"What happened to you?" asked Simone.

"I was shot at", I whispered in her ear, trying desperately to make sure the crowd did not hear me. Though her question had been the same as Yannick Noah's, her reaction to my answer was quite different.

"Quickly", she said to 'Yannick', "bring him into cover", and she started pulling me towards the water-sports pavilion at the top of the beach, which was the nearest building.

"But surely he's joking," said 'Yannick', but he helped Simone to usher me through the curious crowd anyway. I noticed his air of confidence and scorn had cracked a little and he looked about with some nervousness. "No, he isn't joking", Simone responded as we finally got into cover and shut the door on the crowd.

"Could you phone the police please", Simone asked. It occurred to me that we should probably contact Inspector Hoareau rather than the general police but it was too late, they had already phoned Beau Vallon Police Station. After about five minutes, two policemen arrived. Once again I repeated my statement that I was shot at while paragliding. A ghost of a smile crossed the faces of the two policemen but they contained their scepticism better than 'Yannick' had. One asked me how I knew I had been shot at, what had I seen, heard or felt, and I explained as best I could. He continued to look disbelieving. One of them asked 'Yannick' if what I had said was true. He looked at me and then at Simone.

"I don't know", he shrugged, "I couldn't see or hear anything because of the boat."

It was only then that I remembered the severed cord. I told the police and they sent Yannick out to look at his equipment and check if what I had said was correct. He returned looking very nervous and said in a whisper that I was right - I don't know whom he thought would overhear him in that small room. The police appeared to be utterly confused.

"Are you staying at this hotel'?" one of them asked.

"No," Simone replied on my behalf, "we are both staying at the Fisherman's Cove Hotel."

The police both became immediately alert.

"Are you attending the Conference there?" they asked.

Once they knew that I was a Conference delegate their attitude quickly changed. They said they would take us straight to the Fisherman's Cove Hotel so that we could give our story to the Conference Security police. Simone crept out and picked up our bathing gear. She told them that we had a mini-moke in the car park.

Leave it", they said. By this time, Noah looked positively startled.

"Do you mean to say he was shot at?' he asked the police as we left.

"Most probably", the police replied.

"Mon Dieu", he exclaimed. Gradually the look of confidence and superiority returned to his face. What a great story he had·to tell his friends - and the female tourists. His part in it could be made to sound very brave and dramatic. Simone shook his hand and said thanks very much for your help. "I was pleased to help you, madam", he replied and kissed' her hand. "Any time you return I will be pleased to help you again - in any way you wish", he added, with a grin. Simone smiled.

The police drove us back to the Fisherman's Cove Hotel. We forgot all about Mayhew and Virginia. They had been so engrossed in each other that, they had not seen my drama and we had been so engrossed in my drama that we forgot we had taken them to the beach. I had to pacify an angry Mayhew when he eventually got back to the hotel after spending a frustrating two hours looking for Simone and I on the beach and then taking Virginia back to Victoria by taxi.

I was late for my 3 pm meeting with the Minister. Fortunately, he was not there. I left him a message and went to my room to lie down. My body was sore in most places but felt better than I had anticipated after the shock waves went through me when I hit the water. Hoareau came and asked me more questions and then he called a doctor who came to my room and gave me a quick check-up. He said I was in need of nothing but rest, though he gave me some sedatives and painkillers in case I needed them for sleep.

Brian Franklyn called me at 4.30pm and I went to his room. The other members of the New Zealand delegation were there already. The Minister filled us in on some of the events of the day. He had met with the African Ministers and then dined with his Australian and Canadian counterparts. All the Ministers had been called to a special briefing at 3pm. He looked archly at me and said he had not been able to locate me to let me know our 3 pm meeting would be delayed. I didn't say anything at that stage. The Ministers had been advised that it was now known that a number of South Africans were in Seychelles for the purpose of disrupting and, if possible, cancelling the meeting in order to ensure that no resolution imposing anti- South African trade sanctions was passed by the Conference. It was not yet known how many South African agents there were in the Seychelles. Security for the Conference had been stepped up even further. Because of the small size of Seychelles, the security forces were confident that they would identify, isolate and neutralise the South African agents quite quickly. In the meantime, the Ministers had been asked to stress to the other members of their delegations the importance of exercising care and discretion in their movements and co operating fully with security arrangements. We were to advise the Conference security office if we were planning to leave the hotel area and, if they deemed it necessary, they would assign a police officer to accompany us. They recommended that we were not to go out alone but in groups of three or four. They could not say what type of actions the South Africans would use to try and disrupt or side-track the Conference but felt that the Ministers in particular were all likely to be targets. They were now certain that the shooting of the British journalist on Saturday afternoon was the work of this group and that action indicated how serious and ruthless they were. The police were in the course of examining all South Africans on the island and were hopeful of taking some or all of the agents into custody within a few hours. The Conference would then be able to discuss the important matters on its agenda free of threat and intimidation.

We all looked at each other in stunned surprise. I felt physically sick as I realised the reason for what had happened to me that afternoon. "Christ",. exclaimed Graham Sharp, "so much for a few peaceful days in the tropics."

I said, thinking aloud almost, that now that the South African's plot was known, wouldn't they have failed as everyone will be on their guard.

"Not necessarily", Brian Franklyn pointed out. 'The South Africans know they have no hope of getting this Conference to vote against imposing sanctions. Their aim is simply to prevent any sort of resolution being passed, either by getting the Conference called off altogether on security grounds or by fomenting suspicion and disagreement that makes it impossible for the Conference to agree on a resolution. Any means, be it disinformation, disruption, and it seems, even murder, could be· used. They are not out to make friends, but they certainly want to influence people."

He went on to tell us that the Canadian Minister of Finance had told the meeting this afternoon that he had earlier received a telephone call that conveyed a death threat to him if he supported a proposal to impose sanctions. Also, the details of a speech the South African Prime Minister had made that morning in Pretoria had been circulated to the Ministers. In the speech he had said that any country that adopts disinvestment in South Africa or imposes trade sanctions against them could not expect South Africa to sit back and fail to protect its interests. Such. policies against South Africa would be regarded as acts of aggression and would be the subject of immediate and firm retaliation.

"He did not say so specifically", continued Brian Franklyn, "but none of us believe he was talking only about economic retaliation. We are afraid he is also talking about armed retaliation. That may mean little to us in New Zealand as we are nearly nine thousand miles from South Africa but put yourself in the shoes of Lesotho or Swaziland. The South Africans seem to be saying that the Commonwealth better be ready to fight to back up the economic sanctions because South Africa will be prepared to fight to break them. That threat is obviously designed to make countries close to South Africa think again."

There was stunned silence for a while and then some fairly aimless talk about whether the South Africans were bluffing and if they weren't, what it all meant for New Zealand's position. Prior to Franklyn's revelation I had contemplated keeping what had happened to me that afternoon quiet on the ground that there was no need to worry the others. But I thought that someone in the delegation may hear from some other source, such as the Canadians, and I would find it hard to explain why I had kept it quiet. Also, given what the Minister had now told us, the attack on me could imply that the New Zealand delegation had been singled out along with the Canadians as one of the specific targets and I had been the one attacked only because I had been in the most vulnerable position, high in the air over Beau Vallon Bay. You could not get much more vulnerable than that.

So I explained that I had been shot at earlier that afternoon. I also had to explain what paragliding was. All of them were sceptical at first, particularly John Kershaw. "You must have imagined it was a shot," he said, "after all, how do you know what a passing bullet sounds like? It was probably a mosquito". He laughed and looked around the group. He was surprised to find that nobody else was even smiling let alone laughing.

"I was not sure when the first bullet went past whether that was what it really was. It seemed too unlikely a thing to happen to me. But there was not just.one bullet, there were three. The third one cut one of the cords so I had no doubt left," I replied.

They all realised I was serious. I also told them that the Conference Security Office had taken it very seriously. They all became quiet and tense. They realised that what happened to me could easily happen to them and next time the South Africans may not miss.

"Why do you think you were picked on?" asked Brian Franklyn. It was a reasonable question. I was the most junior member of one of the middle-sized delegations at the Conference.

I could not regard myself as important. My injury or even my death would not cause the show to grind to a halt or to change, course. I had been asking myself the same question ever since it had happened - why me?

"There are two possible reasons that have occurred to me", I said. "First, I was the closest person to John Blake when he was shot. The South Africans may think he said something of significance to me before he died. But if that was the reason, they could· have shot me while I was kneeling next to Blake. That would have stopped me passing on anything I had heard.

The second possibility is that they may have singled New Zealand out for special attention and pressure. After all, they can't like us very much now with the rugby tour being cancelled. That was a big blow to their pride and increased their feeling of isolation. I may have simply been the New Zealander who was the easiest target for them today. The second possibility got to them as it put all of them on the hit list. After discussing it for a while, it was agreed that that was the only plausible explanation for someone like me being a target. If it was the correct reason then not only the Minister but every member of the delegation was at risk.

"Well, clearly we will all have to be bloody careful", said the Minister. There were mumbles of agreement. I almost expected the others to say 'hear, hear', as the Minister's colleagues often did in Parliament.

"I'm not going to leave this hotel until the Conference is over," said Graham Sharp, "I don't fancy being a martyr to any cause." The others agreed that this cautious policy made a lot of sense; better to be a live coward than a dead hero had always appealed to me as eminently sensible advice. Leaving the relative security of the hotel in these circumstances wouldn't allow one to be regarded as a hero. You could only be regarded as a fool. Anyway, the Minister had taken any choice I may have had away.

"Right," he said, "lets act on that basis then. None of us are to leave the Conference area unless there is something urgent and crucial that forces you to do so. Then you clear either with me or Sharp and you advise the police and insist on a police escort if they don't offer you one."

Nobody argued with those instructions. I was glad that I had seen some of the island that morning with Simone. A t least I could say that I had sat on the fantastic Beau Vallon Beach for a few hours. It was possible that I would not get another chance. It seemed a crying shame to have to remain cooped up in an hotel when outside the hotel I knew there was some scenery that was amongst the most beautiful in the world and was to be found nowhere else. 'Unique by a thousand miles' was the slogan the Seychelles advertised its scenic attraction under and it was more accurate than many such slogans. Seychelles was also described as a paradise in the tourist literature. If it wasn't paradise, it was as close as one was likely to get to it on earth. To make matters worse, I knew that when I got back to Wellington, all my friends and workmates would be convinced that I was one lucky bastard who had spent a week lazing on the beaches of a tropical island. Nothing I could say would convince them otherwise.

It was quite late when we got around to going over the Minister's speech. He was to speak after lunch on the Monday. This meant he would have been preceded by five other speakers, including the Australian Minister. The tone of the debate on sanctions would have been set by the time it was his turn. We were prepared to make some last minute changes at lunchtime the next day if we had anticipated the mood of the Conference wrongly. The Minister excused the others and said he and I would have dinner in his room and complete the speech. John Kershaw offered to stay and help, which was surprising for him as he usually avoided work wherever possible, but the Minister dismissed his offer brusquely. I felt a little sorry for him - for a second. We had some real fire and brimstone stuff to add to his speech now and the rewrite went well. Little did we know that we would have a lot more to add by lunchtime the next day.

Chapter Three

WE'VE BEEN HERE BEFORE

At the same time as I heard the grim news from Brian Franklyn, Inspector Hoareau and Simon Llewellyn were discussing how to proceed. Llewellyn had been identified at a briefing for the Ministers as a senior officer of the British Security Service who was here, along with a small team, to assist the local security forces. Llewellyn, I found out later, had been born and educated in Rhodesia and had initially been an army officer in that country. He had gone to Britain soon after U.D.I. He was welcomed into the British establishment as they assumed that he had left Rhodesia because he objected to U.D.I. In fact, he had left because he was far-sighted and had no intention of working for black masters.

"It is clear from Blake saying 'niss' that the South Africans are involved in whatever is going on' said Llewellyn. 'I presume you do know that is the South African National Intelligence Service" 'We do know that' Hoareau responded. 'They have been here before. NIS was involved in the failed coup attempt in 1981 led by Mad Mike Hoare. I remember it well."

Llewellyn did not respond. He looked at Hoareau with a look that appeared to be boredom but in fact was a cover for distaste. Hoareau chose to ignore the obvious rudeness and carried on talking. He was still not certain how to take Llewellyn. He knew he did not like him. Llewellyn seemed to have gone out of his way to make himself unlikeable. He had made it very clear that he regarded the Seychellois as inexperienced no- hopers. Still, Hoareau had to work with him, fortunately only for a few days so he decided to studiously ignore Llewellyn's rudeness. If Llewellyn was half as good as he seemed to think he was he could help them a great deal over the next few days. Hoareau was not about to admit it to Llewellyn but his own experience of dealing with terrorists, enemy agents, mercenaries or what¬ ever label one chose to put on this group of South Africans was nil. He had even missed the one prime example of foreign infiltration of his country. He had been overseas in Britain studying when the 1981 attack had occured. However, he was not about to admit this to Llewellyn. It was indicative of Hoareau's lack of experience and worldliness that he did not realise that Llewellyn already knew this. In preparing for the assignment he had not only looked thoroughly into the backgrounds of all the delegates he had also had the backgrounds of the people who would be in charge of security on the Seychelles side carefully investigated. He had not been impressed by what he had found. Hoareau was well-educated but black and without experience. Those were three severe weaknesses in Llwellyn's mind.

'In 1981' continued Hoareau 'a group of about 50 mercenaries flew into Seychelles on a scheduled flight disguised as a group of rugby players and supporters on an end-of season celebration trip. The group was booked to stay for fourteen days in Seychelles and hotels and transport had all been arranged legitimately by unsuspecting travel agents here. An advance group of 4 or 5 people had been in the country for a few weeks previously making logistical arrangements and trying to gather local support. Their aim was to arrest or kill certain of the leaders of Seychelles government and establish a new government here. All but two of them had made it through customs and into the airport security officer decided to search the luggage of one of the last two and found an AK-47. Realising their cover was blown, the other mercenaries took their weapons out of their luggage. They erected a road-block at one end of the airport and attacked the nearby Ponte La Rue Army Barracks. They killed one Seychellois soldier but the attack was unsuccessful and they were forced back to the airport. They took about seventy tourists and airport staff hostage and took over the airport's control tower. The Seychellois police and army surrounded the airport and it was a stalemate for several hours'.

Some hours later, an Air India plane landed at the airport. The mercenaries had had control of the radio system which allowed them communication with aircraft and they persuaded it to land. The Seychelles' forces tried to prevent the plane from landing by blocking one end of the runway and sending flares into the sky. But they could not block the whole runway as the mercenaries controlled the other end. The mercenaries highjacked that plane and forced it to fly most of them back to South Africa. About forty flew out of Seychelles on that plane and they took one dead and several wounded with them. Those few that were left behind were later arrested. The whole attack turned into a fiasco from the South African's viewpoint because of their early discovery at the airport. But the group was large and heavily armed and had it got into the country successfully it could have been a formidable force. There would undoubtedly have been considerable bloodshed and the government could well have been toppled. The 1981 episode- revealed the lengths to which South Africans were prepared to go as it was believed that about half the mercenaries were, or had been, members of of the South African regular military forces. Llewellyn had listened but not responded. He was well aware of the incident. At the time he had been sorry the attempt had failed; he still was.

Hoareau had been glancing at Llewellyn as he spoke. He had noticed that though Llewellyn was still feigning disinterest, he was actually listening closely.

"I think that they may have adopted a similar strategy this time and sent someone in early to establish a base," continued Hoareau, "It wouldn't surprise me if they have again used a couple posing as man and wife in order to try and avoid arousing suspicion'.

"I think you may be right," said Llewellyn, "The South Africans aren't noted for their innovation If something worked reasonably well for them last time they are likely to do exactly the same thing again." For the next few minutes they managed to discuss the implications without trying to score points off each other. They were sure that Blake's reference to 'niss meant the South African Intelligence Service was involved. But they had no idea what the reference to 'grey thing' meant. They agreed they should investigate not only recent arrivals from South Africa but also those who had arrived any time over the last four months.

''How many South Africans come into Seychelles each week?'
Llewellyn asked.

'About 100" Hoareau answered.

'Christ, that means over four months about 1,600 could have come
in. You haven't got enough people to investigate that number of people'
exclaimed Llewellyn.

Hoareau smiled. 'Most of those people are legitimate tourists who
come to Seychelles for a one or two-week holiday and leave. The people
we are interested in are those that arrived some time ago and are still
here. There should be no more than thirty or forty in that situation,' said
Hoareau. One point to me he thought. Though he had kept his temper
under control so far, he was already tired of Llewellyn's patronizing
attitude and his obvious lack of confidence in Hoareau's ability and
intelligence. He gained quiet satisfaction from catching Llewellyn in
an error of logic.

"You keep saying that we will need to investigate all the South
Africans that have come in but did all those involved in 1981 have South
African passports?" asked Llewellyn.

"No," said Hoareau. Llewellyn· had already known the answer and
he thought he had evened the score by scoring a point against Hoareau.
However, Hoareau produced a list that made it obvious he had been
well-aware of the point. The list showed that in 1981, twenty-seven of
the fifty-two people believed to have been involved had South African
passports. The other twenty-five had passports, either legitimate or
forged, from seven other countries: ten British, seven Zimbabwean,
two Irish, including Mike Hoare, two German, two American., one
Austrian and even one Australian.

They agreed that in the light of that, they would need to get
information on all long stay visitors to Seychelles and· try to whittle
the list down by elimination. Most of the foreigners who had been in
Seychelles for a matter of months should be on work assignments that
should be easy to check from work permits or from their employers so
they hoped that the task would not be too daunting or time consuming.
The President was anxious for some quick results. They also agreed that

it would be too big a task to screen all the tourists that had come in over the last two weeks as that would involve about three thousand people. For more recent arrivals therefore, they would concentrate on those that came in on the weekly British Airways flight from South Africa.

They went on to discuss security arrangements for the Conference centre. The discussion was going reasonably well and Hoareau and Llewellyn were working out some of their suspicions about each other when Hoareau happened to raise the death of John Blake.

"I still cannot work out why the South Africans chose Blake as their first target," he said. "After all, there were many more important people they could have shot just as easily. Why Blake?"

"It's not really that surprising," Llewellyn responded to Hoareau's surprise. "Blake was more than a journalist. It is best that I tell you now. He was a member of my British security squad. He had come to Seychelles prior to the rest of the team and with the identity of a journalist in order to check on the security aspects for us from the outside as it were."

Hoareau was stunned. He restrained his desire to scream. In a cool voice he asked Llewellyn "are you saying you sent someone to spy on us?'

"Not to spy, to check you out. What did you expect?' Llewellyn responded icily. That was not his only purpose' he continued but Hoareau could contain his temper no longer and interrupted him.

"You distrusted us so much you had to have your own secret service here. How many more of your men are here that we have not been told about? It's a gross violation of our sovereignty. I hate to think what the President's response will be when I advise him," Hoareau shouted. He had got on his feet and stood threateningly over Llewellyn. Llewellyn did not feel physically intimidated. He almost succumbed to a temptation to 'teach the young, black bastard a lesson but he fought back the impulse. He realised that he had made a bad tactical mistake - the mistake in his mind was not that he had sent his man in secretly but that he had been fool enough to tell Hoareau about it. He was not worried about his working relationship with Hoareau.

They had to work together whether they liked or trusted each other or not. Llewellyn had often worked with people he hated, and who he knew hated his guts also, and with people he didn't trust. In fact, he didn't trust anyone absolutely. What worried him was that the decision to send a man in early had been his. Sure, the message from the British Minister as conveyed to Llewellyn had been to do everything necessary to ensure that there was no security risk to himself or any other Minister at the Conference. But Llewellyn knew that if the Seychelles President complained formally to the British Minister, the Minister would run for cover. He would say, and not be inaccurate or misleading in doing so, that he had issued no such instruction and the Service had unfortunately shown too much_ enthusiasm in carrying out their mission. The service in turn would save themselves by abandoning Llewellyn. It would all be smoothed over with Llewelleyn as the sacrificial scapegoat. That was something he wanted to avoid. He thought, I will need to calm this fellow down. Pi ty, it would have been a good chance to teach him a lesson otherwise.

"Shut up for a moment and let me explain," he said. Hoareau, after continuing to complain for a moment, was quiet, but he was still very angry.

"What we did was standard procedure on our part for these Conferences," Llewellyn said. That wasn't true but Llewellyn was confident that Hoareau would not know that.

'Also' Blake's main role was not to check up on you. There was always a possibility that some terrorist group would take advantage of this gathering of politicians to try and make a point. If it wasn't South Africans it could have been someone else: Libyans, Palestinians, who knows. Blake as a journalist could ferret around looking for stories and at the same time watch out for any unusual actions or groupings of people. I believe he was on to something about the South Africans and that is why they shot him. Unfortunately, he had not passed on whatever it was he knew."

Hoareau was interested in, and partially placated by, what Llewellyn had said. Despite his inward anger, he found himself asking a question. "If Blake knew something that was so important, why on earth did he not pass it on?" he asked.

"There could be a number of reasons. He may not have realised that what he had seen or heard was so significant. But that doesn't seem likely given his attempts to pass some information on through White. Those few words he got out show clearly that he knew he was dealing with South Africans. Unfortunately, he couldn't pass the information on to you or any of your men as I had told him to work under cover'. Llewelleyn stopped to see if Hoareau would react but he remained silent this time.

Llewellyn continued, "It seems therefore that the young fool was trying to boost his own career by uncovering the group and tried to go too far on his own. I'm· afraid that it happens all too often among young agents, I think they have read too many spy thrillers." He shook his head in mock concern, but at the same time he watched Hoareau closely. It galled him to admit to Hoareau that his men may not always be perfect at their job but he needed to calm Hoareau dcwn. It seemed that his explanation had placated Hoareau to some degree so he carried on while he had the initiative. "I think you should report to your President that on the basis of the comments Blake made to White before he died we think he had found something out about the South Africans. Unfortunately for him, the South Africans were aware that he had and eliminated him. There is nothing to be gained however in telling your President that Blake was one of my agents. He could have found out his information and become, a threat to the South Africans just as easily as a journalist as an agent. We have to work together. The South Africans would be delighted if they managed to cause an argument between your President and my Minister by killing Blake. That would be a real bonus for them."

Hoareau had to admit that that was right. He felt that he was letting Llewellyn off a hook that he did not deserve to get off. But the avoidance of unnecessary argument and tension amongst the Conference delegates was more important than his dislike of Llewellyn. So he decided to accept Llewellyn's compromise, though he did not tell him so. I'll let him stew for a bit longer Hoareau thought.

"What about White?" he went on. "Why do you think the South Africans are trying to kill hjm?"

"I've been thinking about that too," said Llewellyn. He thought that the fact that Hoareau had shifted from the other issue to ask about White meant that he was off the hook on the Blake problem. He was grateful for that but his gratitude was not directed at Hoareau. Llewellyn hated anyone else having something on him. It put him in a position of potential weakness and that was a position he did not like. I'll have to watch this bastard he thought to himself. I'll have to try and get something on him in order to neutralise the significarnce of what he knows. In the meantime I will have to treat him gently. Llewellyn was sure that Hoareau would have been thinking along similar, but opposite, lines. It would have come as a profound shock to him if he had known that Hoareau had no such thoughts.

"At first I thought that they may have realised or suspected that Blake had passed something on to White before he died, something that could identify some of them. But if that was their motivation, they would not have waited eighteen hoursto make an attempt on his life," continued Llewellyn. "They would have shot him as he knelt beside Blake, so there must be another reason."

A thought suddenly occurred to Hoareau, "It could be that White is a New Zealand security service officer. If you have undercover agents at the Conference, maybe some of the other delegations have also." He enjoyed the opportunity to rub salt in Llewellyn's embarrassment.

"It is possible that some of the delegations do have such people," Llewellyn responded, "but I do not think the New Zealanders would be one of them. They don't go in for much of that sort of thing and if they did they would have informed us'. Damn, I've put my foot in it again, thought Llewellyn. I'll have to stop talking so much. The best way to make sure you don't say the wrong thing is to say nothing. That was one of the rules of behaviour that Llewellyn customarily acted upon. Hoareau had somehow managed to make him forget the rule for a while. Llewellyn determined not to repeat the mistake again.

"If that's not the reason, then what is it?" asked Hoareau.

Llewellyn thought carefully before he answered and, when he started, he spoke slowly and carefully.

"I think it is quite simple really. The South Africans want to build up a climate of fear and suspicion. They would dearly love to have the

Conference called off early because of inadequate security or even just have some delegations leave for that reason. That would be why they shot Blake in such a public place. They obviously could have taken him out quietly but chose to do it where it would have the maximum impact on the nerves of the delegates. They probably see New Zealand as a crucial intermediary between the hard line States of the Commonwealth who want to isolate South Africa entirely and bring it to its knees, and the older dominions who, they hope, may continue to argue against sanctions or at least water down any· sanctions that are imposed until they become meaningless as anything other than a gesture. I think White became a target by chance. He was the New Zealander who was most easily available. Fancy going paraglidi9ng in these circumstances. The guy has no sense at all.'

"You are probably right. But given that the South Africans are usually expert marksmen - they hit Blake with a single shot from a considerable distance - I wonder if they were actually trying to kill White. It seems more likely to me that they were only out to give him a fright so that he would come back here and pass his fear on to the rest of the New Zealanders. He will have done that. I think we should have a talk to either their Minister or one of the senior officials to see if they have had any other threats and to see what their reaction is going to be to White's experience," said Hoareau.

Llewellyn agreed. They discussed the procedures they should adopt to get the various steps they proposed to take under way. The investigation of South Africans and other long stay visitors had to take priority. Ideally they would like to have something of substance that the President could inform the Conference about when it opened tomorrow. Talking to the New Zealanders was of secondary importance but Llewellyn said he would arrange to do that in the morning. Llewellyn was anxious to know what Hoareau intended to do about his revelation of Blake's role. In the end, against his better judgement, he could stand the uncertainty no longer and asked Hoareau. Hoareau casually responded that he had not yet decided. He would make up his mind when he next spoke to the President. Llewellyn fumed inwardly but could do or say nothing.

Hoareau enjoyed observing his discomfort. They parted on more or less amicable terms, on the surface, and Hoareau proceeded to set in train the preparation of the list of foreigners resident in Seychelles that would need to be investigated.

Chapter Four

TOO CLOSE FOR COMFORT

We finished the redraft of the Minister's speech at about 9 pm. He said he was going to read through it one more time but said I could go. He was going to put a call through to the Prime Minister at 10 pm, when it would be 8 am on Monday morning in Wellington, to get his approval on the line he wanted to take on the sanctions. He did not think he would have any difficulty getting the Prime Minister's approval but he was not prepared to move without it.

I decided to go down to the hotel bar for a nightcap or two. A number of delegates were there, including a group of the younger ones who had once again gravitated to each other. Simone Lablache was there, but before I could join the group she was in, I was buttonholed by Andrew Mayhew.

"Peter, could you please come and have a drink with me. I need to talk to you," he said. Normally I would have made some excuse and gone to join Simone but having already offended Mayhew once today, I thought I had better listen to him. He ordered us drinks and then he said to me, "What do you think of Virginia?"

It was easy to say that she was one of the most beautiful women I had ever seen and that she also seemed to be a nice person. I didn't have to make them up. Both comments were true.

Mayhew nodded his head in agreement. "I think I am in love with her' he said.

I began to smile but then I saw he was deadly serious.

"I don't blame you at all," I said. 'You could look for ever to find someone better and from what I saw, she probably feels the same way about you."

"Do you think so?" Mayhew asked, but he did not wait for an answer before continuing. "I wonder how she would fit in in England. It would be a different way of life to what she is used to. Would she be happy there or would she pine for the Seychelles."

"What are you really concerned about?" I asked, "Is it whether she will enjoy England and fit in or is it that you are not sure if English people will accept her?" I may have been too blunt but he was not taken aback.

"Well, it's a bit of both," he said. "I'm sure she will be accepted by my friends. The English aren't as snobbish as you think and they will be charmed by her in the same way I have been. But I am not sure what my family's reaction will be. You see my grandfather lived in Seychelles as a British colonial administrator early this century. My grandmother was with him initially, but she did not like it and returned to England. My grandfather took a Seychellois woman as a live-in housekeeper and ended up living with her as man and wife. The family never forgave him. I am not sure therefore what their reaction would be if I returned with a Seychellois woman.'

"Well, there is only one way to find out. Take her to England," I said.

"I don't know," he said. "I have got used to living alone and I actually enjoy it. But the thought of going away from Seychelles and leaving Virginia here makes me very depressed. You know, she even gave me a beautiful old leather briefcase that had been her grandfather's and which he had passed on through her father to her. But she said she would be happiest if I was using it as then I would always have something with me when we were apart to remind me of her. She is someone special. I've never felt this way about anyone before and I'm not sure what I should do."

"It's my opinion that you would rank as the biggest idiot of all time," I said, "if you let her get away from you."

"Do you really think so?" he said.

I nodded and suggested that the only way to find out for himself was to ask Virginia.

"Let's go and join the others," I said before he had a chance to ask me anything further. Love may be beautiful but it can also be a bore if you are the unfortunate third party that one of the lovers chooses to share their desires and doubts with.

I led the way to the group that Simone was in. She had obviously been telling the others about our afternoon experience. I was asked as soon as I arrived to tell the story again from my perspective - what was it like to be shot at they all wanted to know. I was surprised to find that I enjoyed telling the story. Like a lot of things; it seemed more exciting and less disturbing in retrospect than it had at the time. Eight hours after it had happened, I could look back and convince myself {almost) that I had acted with great calmness and cleverness 'under fire'. At least, that was how it sounded as I retold the events. The others seemed to be suitably impressed, especially as Simone backed up my new version of how things had happened and gave a clear impression that I had handled it very well. We talked for some time about the seriousness of the South African threat to the Conference.

The general consensus of this group was that with the plot uncovered and security stepped up, there was little more the South Africans would be able to do and we probably would not hear much more about their threats at this Conference. Ah, the confidence - and inexperience - of youth.

Simone's room and my room were on the same floor of the hotel so we went upstairs together. She invited me to have a coffee in her room, an invitation I willingly accepted. She phoned room service for coffee for two while I made myself comfortable in one of her chairs. The rooms we were in were quite small and quite sparsely furnished, particularly when compared with the relative luxury of the Ministerial suites upstairs. I contemplated sitting on the end of one of the two ·beds but thought she might regard that as a bit forward.

She asked me if I would like a port with my coffee. "I have a very nice South African port that I got duty free in Mauritius," she said. "South African?" I said with surprise. She laughed. I had taken the bait. She was pulling my leg. The port was from Portugal. She poured two ports and brought one to me. She then went over to the window to pull the curtains. Suddenly, she gasped and rushed back from the window into my arms. Just as I was thinking that my charms had never worked that quickly before she whispered 'there is someone out on one of the other balconies. 'I said it is probably just someone taking some night air.

"No," she whispered. "The person is all in black and he is climbing from balcony to balcony coming in this direction.' I had to admit that did not sound like someone innocently taking some night air. I turned off the light and went and peered carefully through the curtains. She was right. There was someone all in black clothes and who seemed to have black or blackened skin as well. He (I presumed it was a he) was quite eerie. And he was coming in the direction of Simone's room. I was immediately convinced that he was after me again. It did not occur to me that I was in Simone's room rather than my own and that the assailant, whomever he was, would not know that. I hadn't known myself until two minutes ago that that was where I would be. I returned over to where Simone was standing, holding on to the dressing table. I asked her to phone the hotel security watch-room while I tried to keep an eye on the prowler without being seen myself. As I watched through the curtains, the prowler climbed on to a balcony only three or four rooms down from ours and then disappeared. I cautiously edged my head out still further but could no longer see him. Just then there was a quiet knock on the door. We both reacted as if a gun had gone off. Simone recovered first and went and whispered through the door 'who's there?' I didn't hear the response but she opened the door. Two police officers came in very quietly. There were more in the corridor. I explained that the prowler had disappeared off the balcony three or four rooms to the right. It seemed most likely that he had gone into a room. The police told us to lock the door again after they had gone and went out of the room and moved quietly down the corridor to the right. They took up positions outside the room where I thought the prowler had gone and the rooms on either side as well, just in case my sense of distance had been mistaken. They had keys that would open any of the room doors. They opened all three doors simultaneously and rushed into the rooms. There were some very startled conference delegates, one of whom was n a very compromising situation with a local prostitute.

I was still peering through the curtains. All of a sudden, the prowler rushed out the room he was in and on to the balconies again and started to cross the balconies in my direction. He saw that the window to our room was open and the lights were off. Probably assuming that either the room was empty or the occupant was asleep, he suddenly changed direction and rushed through the curtains into the room. I tackled him as he came through the curtains - or to be honest, he came in so surprisingly and fast that I couldn't get out of his way in time. Still, Simone was convinced when she retold the story later to the police that I had deliberately tackled the intruder and far be it for me to argue with her version of events.

As he hit the floor, I realised that the intruder had a knife. It slipped out of his hand when he fell and skidded across the floor and under the chair I had been sitting on a few peaceful minutes ago. The intruder, unfortunately, had also seen where it had gone and crawled rapidly across the floor and retrieved it. I had been too shaken by this sudden turn of events to move. Simone kept perfectly still and quiet. His tumble had not seemed to have hurt the intruder - only anger and frighten him. He stood up and started coming slowly towards me. I was mesmerised by the knife in his hand. It looked huge - both the hand and the knife. Huge and deadly. I realized in the pit of my stomach that I had a greater fear of knives than of guns. Guns seemed impersonal and their actions when they were used were so quick that one had no time to anticipate the consequences. But knives were very personal, almost an extension of the knife-wielders arm. The build up to their action was slow and deliberate. It gave the would-be victim, in this case me, plenty of time to contemplate what lay ahead and to anticipate the tearing of skin, muscle, and vital organs. I had never fainted before in my life but at that moment I came as close to it as I ever had. I would have been relieved if I had fainted but all that happened was that. I was swept by a wave of nausea. I may well have been physically sick if Simone had not been present, but I fought back the nausea to avoid embarrassment in her eyes. I retreated slowly towards the balcony as the intruder came inexorably onward. He had got such a shock when he came into what he thought was an empty room, and had focussed his intention subsequently so fixedly on retrieving his knife and stalking me, that he had not realised that there was anyone else in the room. Simone had kept her cool very well. She was a very sensible person, fortunately for me.

As I watched and tried to show no reaction, she quietly picked up the bottle of port from the side table, crept up behind the intruder, who was still so intent on me that he was oblivious to anything else, and she hit him over the head with the bottle. He went down for the second and last time. She had hit him so hard that the bottle broke. I turned the lights on and gave Simone a quick hug.

My God, you are marvellous I thought. I could still vividly imagine the feel of that knife as it entered my stomach. My stomach muscles had tensed up so much that I actually felt as if I had been stabbed and I had difficulty standing up straight. My face and body were covered in sweat.

We looked at the intruder as we continued to hold each other. The first thing I noticed was that he was not going to move for a while. This did not surprise me given the blow that Simone had given him. The second thing I noticed, with some surprise this time, was that he was African - that is to say a black African, not a white South African.

We had no time to ponder the significance of that fact. The police unlocked the door to Simone's room and came into the room on the run with guns in their hands. Fortunately, they looked rather than fired first. As the people outside in the corridor realised that all seemed to be quiet in the room, a number of curious onlookers followed the police into the room. It soon became crowded. We explained briefly to the police what had happened in the room. We gathered from them and the comments of the onlookers that someone had been stabbed in one of the other rooms. We found out later that it was one of the Ministers - the Minister of Finance for the Gambia - and that he had died instantly. Just then Hoareau arrived and took charge of proceedings. The police dragged the intruder roughly to his feet and took the knife from his hands. It no longer looked so big somehow. The intruder, or murderer as he could now be called, began to come round. He struggled briefly and half-heartedly. The police had him securely in their grip. They turned him towards the door. There was a gasp from one of the onlookers clustered near the door.

I know him," said the man.

"Shut up," Hoareau snapped. "You stay here." He grabbed the person who had spoken. "The rest of you go back to your rooms.'

He shouted "Now!" when none of them moved. They were all

hustled out of the room, except the one who said he recognised the murderer, and the door was closed.

"Now," said Hoareau to the person who remained, "who are you and who do you say he is?"

"I am Doctor Gabriel Rawene," he said with pride. 'He is Samson Aminu, a junior member of our delegation." "Which delegation?" asked Hoareau.

"The Gambian delegation," answered Rawene.

"What?", exclaimed the startled Hoareau. "It was your Minister who has been murdered. Are you telling me he has murdered his own Minister?'

It was Dr Rawene's turn to be startled. "What do you mean by the murder of his Minister? What has happened to Mr Bangura?" He reeled towards Samson Aminu. 'What have you done?" he shouted.

Hoareau realised that Rawene had been unaware that a murder had been committed and the Gambian Minister had been the victim. Hoareau had arrived late on the scene and had not been certain what had been said before he arrived. He grabbed Rawene by the arm and led him to one of the chairs. He was more concerned about what Rawene might try to do to Aminu when he found out what had happened than he was solicitious of Rawene's state of mind.

"Your Minister was stabbed in his room just a few minutes ago," he said. "I am sorry to have to tell you but he died instantly. This man you say is Samson Aminu rushed out of the Minister's room and was apprehended in this room. We have every reason to believe he was the murderer."

Rawene tried to stand but was restrained by Hoareau's firm hand on his shoulder. He turned towards Aminu and glared at him. If looks could kill, Aminu would have been a dead man.

"Do you mean to tell me that you are working for the South Africans?" asked Rawene, in a voice filled with shock and despair.

"Like hell," growled Aminu, "This has nothing to do with the South Africans."

"Then why?" asked Rawene. But Aminu didn't reply. He hung his·head and remained mute.

"None of you are to say anything to anyone about this until you have been interviewed by security. Is that clear?" said Hoareau in his sternest voice. Then he realised that he was talking to foreign officials to the Conference and said in a more placating tone, "I trust you will understand the necessity for what I have asked. We need to try and establish exactly what has happened and, just as importantly, why it happened. We should not jump to conclusions even though things look clear cut. Once we have established the facts we will inform all the Conference delegates. It would be unfortunate if misleading versions of the events were spread first."

That made sense to me. I was in no mood to argue and neither was Simone or the still shell-shocked Gambian official.

"I will have to talk to the other members of my delegation," Rawene said haltingly. 'They need to be advised. I will also need to tell the President in Gambia. We will need to decide what we should do in response both here and in my country."

Hoareau thought for a while. He then agreed that what Dr Rawene wished to do was appropriate. But he stressed that Rawene should just pass on the known facts - that the Minister had been stabbed to death and that one of the younger members of the Gambian delegation was being held on strong suspicion of being responsible. To the rest of us he repeated that we should not talk about it to anyone before we were given the appropriate approval of security. He obviously changed his mind for just ten minutes after the police had ushered Aminu out of Simone's room and Hoareau had left, he was back.

Hoareau apologised for disturbing us again but they needed to make sure that they understood exactly what we had seen and what had happened in this room before they questioned Aminu. They thought it would be most efficient, for them and for us, if they talked to Simone and I together.

We described the events in sequence. Simone gave a glowing description of my tackling the intruder. Gave a glowing description of her attack on the intruder, which I was sure had saved my life. We were a mutual admiration society. There was not much beyond the sequence of events that we could tell them. The thing that was most puzzling was the motive, but on that Simone and I had nothing to contribute.

I asked Inspector Hoareau if he could explain what was going on - where did this murder fit in to the South African plots? At first I thought he was not going to reply. However, after thinking about it, he decided to share his views with us. He said they did not yet know the reasons for this murder but it was his suspicion that Aminu had decided to take advantage of the South African threat to carry out some private business of his own. He would have hoped that he would have got away unobserved and that suspicion would have fallen on the South Africans. The motive for the murder probably lay back in the Gambia and they did not know if it was a political attack or a personal grudge. Once they were sure that the case was unrelated to the threats against the Conference, they would probably not waste time on Aminu. They had more serious things to investigate. They would leave the investigating of Aminu's actions and his fate to the authorities in the Gambia.

"Unfortunately," concluded Hoareau, "whatever the motive, the murder will increase tension at this Conference and this will indirectly help the South Africans in their aims. It will certainly make our security task more difficult. In view of that please keep the attack on you at Beau Vallon Beach quiet. There is no need to alarm the Ministers and other delegates more than necessary. Also, would you please not talk to other delegates about tonight's events until such time as the Chairman makes a formal statement to the Conference, probably first thing tomorrow. I would also like to congratulate the two of you on the way you handled the attack by Aminu. This whole situation could have been much worse if you had not succeeded in knocking him out."

Well, having been taken into Hoareau's confidence and praised for our actions as well, how could we possibly disagree with what he asked of us. I did tell him that I had already told the rest of the New Zealand delegation about the shots that had been fired at me at Beau Vallon Bay. Both Simone and I forgot about our conversation in the bar earlier in the evening.

As he was leaving, Hoareau remarked with a grin that it was

fortunate that we had both been in the same room. If there had only been one person in the room, who knows what might have happened.

It was about 11 pm when Hoareau and his colleague left. We never had the coffee or port. The coffee never arrived and the port was spread over the floor of the room. Most probably the waiter who brought the coffee took it away again when he discovered Simone's room full of policemen. I wondered what rumours may have been circulating among the staff. The port was spread liberally around the room from the shattering of the bottle on Aminu's head. It leant a heady aroma to the atmosphere in the room. We picked up the obvious pieces of broken glass and made a preemptory attempt to mop up the port but soon gave up.

I said it was late and that I had better be going back to my room. Two attacks in one day was more than I was used to, and with the conference starting tomorrow, we both needed some sleep. Simone looked at me for a moment and then she glanced at the window, and then back to me. She said that she was afraid to be alone. She was sure she would not be able to sleep at all if she was on her own. As soon as she closed her eyes, she would visualise knife-wielding intruders flooding through her window. Every night sound outside, and there were lots of them - dogs, frogs, cats, bats, bar sounds, car sounds - would convince her that another intruder was lurking outside.

She was very convincing. She didn't need to have made such a strong case. Most of the time I was capable of taking a hint. I asked her if she would like me to stay the night in her room. She walked slowly into my arms and held me tight and repeated 'yes, yes

"You undress in here, I'll go into the bathroom," said Simone. She seemed momentarily embarrassed by her display of emotions. I thought that undressing separately was a little coy but I nodded in agreement.

There was no need to rush things and certainly no need to argue about it. I remembered how good Simone had looked in her swimsuit that morning and thought that after all my trials and tribulations during the day something good was going to come out of the day after all.

I realised that I should have asked her if I could shower before things got this far as I was sweating profusely. I crept over to her dressing table and looked through her cosmetics. I smeared some deodorant on my armpits and sprayed some perfume on my body. That would have to do.

I quickly undressed. I climbed into the bed nearest the bathroom door. I was thinking about what move I would make should Simone get into the other bed when she came quietly out of the bathroom. She was wearing a nightie, to my surprise, but I saw that it left little to my imagination. I held out one hand and she came to me and took my hand. I turned back thebedclothes and made room for her to get in. She gasped a little when she saw I was nude, but her eyes sparkled and she smiled. "I had nothing to wear," I said. "Besides it is hot in the Seychelles."

"It is hot, isn't it," she replied and dropped her nightie and climbed in beside me. We kissed eagerly and ran our hands over each other's bodies. I kissed her lips, her cheeks, her neck and her breasts. We were both quickly excited and made love with urgency and passion. She gasped as I entered her and her fingers ran up and down my spine, tearing at the skin, as we thrust together. Her nails were sharp and it hurt but it added to my excitement. I reached my climax quickly - too quickly I suspected for Simone. I felt exhausted by the effort. It was as if I had run ten miles. It had been a long and most unusual day, however, so I felt I had some excuse.

We lay together afterwards, talking quietly. Simone was clearly not satisfied and she caressed me tenderly but persistently while we talked. Gradually my tired body reacted to the sensations of her touch. This time our love-making was slower, less hectic and longer. When it was over we both lay back, tired and satisfied. This time we didn't talk. I soon fell asleep.

Chapter Five

YES MINISTER

I woke at 6.30 on Monday morning. I was habitually an early waker. It must have been something to do with spending my childhood and early years on a New Zealand dairy farm. For ten months of the year one woke at 5.30 am to get up and milk those bloody cows, seven days a week. After doing this for several years, no matter what time I had got to bed the night before or the condition I was in on going to bed I automatically woke up about ten seconds before the alarm clock went off every morning, or almost every morning. There were the occasional mornings when too much drink the night before or a particularly exciting dream seemed to dull the mechanism of my mental alarm. So I was never confident enough to do without a mechanical back up from the infernal alarm clock. Somehow I always felt less rested and more irritable when the alarm clock shook me awake than when I woke myself. It was fifteen years since I had got up regularly to milk cows but the habit of my mental alarm clock waking me early persisted. Fortunately, it went off at around 6.30am these days.

I tended to be an early starter compared with most other staff in the Minister's office and arrived at work before 8 am. It was amazing how many of the small but necessary tasks one could get done in an hour when there were few other people around to interrupt you and, even more importantly, the damn telephone didn't ring. Despite the excitements of the night before my mental alarm clock quietly woke me at 6.30am. For a while I was confused by my surroundings. I was in a strange bed. I always wake with that feeling momentarily whenever I am in a hotel bed, or any other bed than my own. I was also in a strange room and there was someone else in the bed with me. As I slowly made the journey from unconsciousness to consciousness, I recalled the events of the last night. I shuddered as I remembered some, I smiled as I remembered others. Simone was still sleeping soundly. I crept out of bed as carefully as I could. Simone stirred and rolled over but she did not wake up. I dressed quietly and quickly. I wrote Simone a short note to tell her that I had woken early and gone back to my room in case someone had been trying to get in contact with me. I said I would see her at the Conference opening session. I was not sure how to close the note. I wanted to say something affectionate but did not want to overdo it after just one night together. So I closed it simply with love, Peter, and tiptoed out the door.

There was a policeman sitting on a chair in the corridor outside the door. Police had been placed in all the hotel corridors after last night's murder but I did not know that at the time. I thought he had been put there especially to keep an eye on us. I was both startled and embarrassed by his presence, but he gave me a· broad grin. There may even have been the hint of a wink but I could not be sure. He cheerily said "bonjour monsieur." I mumbled good morning in reply and hurried down the corridor to my room. As I opened the door I glanced back in his direction. He was still looking at me - and he was still grinning broadly. Ah what the heck I thought and smiled back.

I entered my room and pulled the curtains - very slowly. You cautious fool I thought, last night has shaken your nerve. Whereas the scene outside the windows had in the dark of last night appeared sinister, with every shadow suspicious and every noise malevolent, in the clear light of morning the scene could not have looked more peaceful. The sun was shining brightly and the gardens looked very tropical. The ever-present coconut palms were looking majestically down on a colourful array of hibiscus, bouganvillia, flame trees, mango, paw-paws and bananas. There were a number of large granite boulders strewn around the garden and orchids clambered up them. Most people raved about the beauty of orchids but I was not that impressed. The flowers were delicate and intricate but I did not always find the shape pleasing - I preferred a more straight forward, simple flower like a daffodil. But the orchid plant had nothing to recommend it other than the flower that it held. It was a stringy, spindly, ugly excuse for a plant. There were already local women out raking up the leaves - they seemed to have an aversion to leaves lying on the ground in Seychelles and were forever raking them up and·burning them. I wondered why they burnt them rather than using them as compost or mulch.

Without really thinking why I had done it, or who I was trying to fool, I turned back the bedclothes on one of the beds and ruffled the blankets to try and give the impression that someone had slept in the bed. Then I noticed that there was a message on the dressing ·table. It asked me to ring the Minister. It was timed at 10.50 pm last night. It was now eight hours later. I knew the Minister was an early riser like me. As it was then just after 7.00. I decided to get the task over with and phoned his room straight away - better late than never I hoped.

"Where the hell were you last night?" he grumbled after I had said good morning sir in as cheery voice as I could muster. I seldom called him sir. I was obviously feeling on the defensive.

'I tried to get you about 10. 30 and you weren't in your room. They paged the bar and you weren't there. Where were you?" Fortunately he was eager to continue talking and didn't give me a chance to answer the question.

"I spoke to the Prime Minister by phone last night and not only did he fully support my line, he thought we should go even further. He is going to discuss the issue with Cabinet at a special meeting but he is sure Cabinet will back him up. They always do on issues like this. We will need to contact him again later this morning for confirmation and final instructions. I had to rewrite large sections of the speech myself when I couldn't locate you. I got some help from Sharp and Barnes but what is the point of bringing you along as a speech writer if you are not around when the writing needs to be done." I was just about to try and offer some sort of explanation, not necessarily the whole truth however, but he carried on talking. "I have two versions of some sections of the speech," he said, "as there won't be time for a major rewrite between your talk with the Prime Minister and my speech this afternoon."

"My talk with the Prime Minister?" I managed to ask.

"Yes, you will need to phone him. But let's not waste any more time. Come up to my room now and we will go over the rewrites." It was clear from the tone of his voice that he was not pleased with me. He was not an excessively demanding boss, at least compared with a number of other politicians who expected their staff to be around at all hours of the day and night.

This was my first trip overseas with the Minister, I had the uneasy feeling that unless I was more careful I could succeed in making it my last one also. I hurried to his room, after tidying myself up quickly. I apologised for my absence last night and explained my involvement in the attack and murder of the Gambian Minister of Finance. I realised that Hoareau had asked me not to talk about the incident but I thought it would be safe to tell the Minister. It would have been very difficult to explain my absence without mentioning it. I decided to keep quiet about where I was for the rest of the night, however.

The Minister had not heard about the murder and was understandably alarmed and shocked. He had not known Thomas Bangura, the murdered Minister, well, but he regarded all the Commonwealth Ministers of Finance as colleagues. He assumed that it was the work of the South Africans and was alarmed that they could gain access to the hotel. He wondered who the next target would be. I think he was feeling nervous about his own position.

I forgot my undertaking to Inspector Hoareau and before I remembered I had told the Minister that it was not the South Africans, the murderer was another Gambian. The police did not know what the motive was but believed it was internal to Gambian politics. I concluded that I did not think it constituted a threat to any other Ministers. He was relieved to hear it. It was only at that stage that I recalled my undertaking to Hoareau not to talk about it. I thought of telling the Minister but decided to take the risk that he wouldn't talk about it to anyone else. I didn't want to appear unreliable in his eyes for a second time. I assumed it was only a matter of a short time, before the Conference Chairman would make all that I had told the Minister common knowledge. The Minister said that I seemed to be displaying a penchant for being in the wrong place at the wrong time. I had to agree with him.

He went on to tell me the details of his conversation with the Prime Minister and we went quickly over the second version of his speech that had been drafted last night. The content was fine but some parts of it did not sound like the Minister's style - or at least his style as I write it. I suggested that I reword two or three of the paragraphs and he agreed. He said he was going to have breakfast. As penance for not being around, I could stay and do the redrafting. I did not feel I was in a position to argue.

Brian Franklyn was to speak immediately after lunch that day. The afternoon session did not start until 3.00pm. They have long lunch sessions at these conferences. The older delegates assured me when I pointed this out that there were good reasons for the long break. They claimed that the most effective diplomatic work and lobbying was done in discussions over lunch rather than in the formal conference sessions which tended to be set pieces. Also, they frequently scheduled sub-committee meetings for the lunch break. I was still working in his room when the Minister returned from breakfast. He gave me my instructions on when and how I was to contact the New Zealand Prime Minister's office. In order to ensure that I had a safe line, it had been arranged for me to phone from the British High Commission office in Victoria. Telephones at the conference venue were supposed to be safe, and probably were, but the Minister wanted to be sure. It was not only South Africans he was thinking about. There were a lot of journalists around the hotel and he did not want any premature leaks of the New Zealand position.

I was told that I would need to phone at 11 am Seychelles time which would be 9 pm in Wellington. The Prime Minister's office would be waiting for my call at that time. A police escort had been arranged to take me to Victoria and the High Commission would be expecting me and would have the line ready.

"You see," said the Minister, "while you were off playing cops and robbers last night, some of us were working." He grinned as he said it. I was glad I had not told him where I had been for the rest of the night. His tone would have been much more sarcastic had he known.

He said he was off to talk to the Australian Minister. He was so bouyed up by the anticipation of his speech that he actually ruffled my hair affectionately as he went past. That was most unusual for him. He was generally friendly with his staff but on a surface level only. He was seldom personal. His action took me by surprise and I did not respond in time. By the time its significance dawned on me he had left the room. I thought I actually heard him whistling as he left. That too was most unusual. He was not usually the whistling type.

Chapter Six

NIGHT RAIDS

We were not the only early risers that morning. Hoareau and Llewellyn were out and about much earlier than the Minister and I had been. nThey had spent the early part of Sunday night going through the list of all South Africans and some visitors of other nationalities who had stayed in Seychelles for a month or more. There were forty-two names on the initial list. They had by enquiry from various officials who should have had contact with the people concerned if their reasons for being in Seychelles were genuine, managed to eliminate most of them from the list. By midnight there were only three couples left on the list who had not been cleared. There were a lot of worried Seychellois officials however who wondered what was wrong with their foreign colleague that warranted a police check-up in the middle of the night. Some of the suspicions generated lingered on for a long time.

If the South Africans had been long-sighted and clever and devious they may have set their agents up with a sound cover based on some legitimate job in the Seychelles under a non-South African identity. In that case this quick screening process would have missed them. Both Hoareau and Llewellyn realised there was a risk of this but in the time available they could not be any more thorough. Besides, the South Africans had not been noted for their subtlety in their previous covert operations. Indeed, subtlety did not seem to be one of the characteristics of the South African personality. So they were relying on the South Africans sending in their advance agents with a minimum of cover.

Once the three couples had been identified, Hoareau had left the arrangements regarding raids on their houses to his assistant, Phillipe Auguste, and Llewellyn for a period. He had been informed about the murder of Thomas Bangura and muttering "that was all that he needed right now," he had left to interview the assailant and to talk to White and Lablache. It struck him as curious how often he ended up talking

55

to these two, but he had realised from childhood that some people were more accident prone than others - it seemed to him that White was one of those. Hoareau soon realized that this murder was a diversion as far as his main preoccupation with the South African agents was concerned. The senior ranking officer of the Gambian delegation had told him that the delegation intended to leave the Conference and return home to brief the government. They had no desire to remain at "the scene of this act of shame for our country" he had said. Hoareau had told him that he had no objections to that from the police point of view and they could discuss the matter with the Conference authorities. Hoareau realised that some of the delegation members may be material witnesses in the murder enquiry but he had no desire to carry out that enquiry. Enquiries with political overtones were always difficult - doubly so when the overtones came from some other country's politics.

The Gambian official had already spoken by phone to his Prime Minister, who was also head of police and security matters in his country. The Prime Minister had asked him to inform the Seychelles authorities that the Gambians would be requesting extradition of Samson Aminu for trial in the Gambia even though the crime had been committed in the Seychelles. Hoareau had told him that they would hold Aminu until the extradition request had been formally received and dealt with. Personally, Hoareau would be very happy to wipe his hands of the matter, put Aminu on a plane to Gambia and let the Gambians deal with their own dirty linen. He had then briefly questioned Peter White and Simone Lablache. He had not really expected to learn anything new or startling from them. He hoped that what they had to say would allow him to safely put any further investigation of this incident aside and return to the main investigation. He was satisfied that he could do so.

He had driven from his talk with White and Lablache to the State House in Victoria. The President, Albert Baptiste had asked for a security briefing, even though it was now after midnight. President Baptiste would be formally opening the Conference the following morning and he would need to inform the Conference of what had happened and what the security forces were doing - in broad terms at least. Hoareau reviewed the situation in his mind as he was driven to Victoria. All that they knew was that they were now sure that South African agents were present in Seychelles, that the murder of Thomas Bangura was an unrelated incident, that the death of Blake was almost certainly due to the South Africans, as was the attack on White, and that an explicit threat had been received by the Canadian delegation and an implicit one by the New Zealand delegation. He also knew why Blake had been eliminated by the South Africans but he decided not to tell that to the President as he feared Baptiste's reaction to the knowledge that the British had been in effect, spying on them would be extreme and they could do without extreme reactions at present.

What they did not know was how many agents there were or who any of them were. Those were fairly big gaps in their knowledge. What were they doing to plug those gaps? Their investigation of recent visitor arrivals in Seychelles had not revealed any suspicious large group of arrivals like the 1981 group: no rugby teams, soccer teams, diving groups, rotary club groups or any other likely cover aggregation of reasonably fit-looking, predominantly male groups coming from South Africa or anywhere else for that matter. On the basis of that, Hoareau decided to stick his neck out and tell the President that they believed the group to be relatively small - say five to ten people at most. Llewellyn had agreed that that was probably a reasonable assumption. He would outline to the President their investigation of long-term visitors to Seychelles, their belief that the South Africans would probably have sent in an advance team, and their plan to raid three houses of suspects early in the morning. He would need the President's approval for the raids because of any repercussions that might follow if innocent people got hurt.

On the basis of the raids, he was going to tell the President that he was confident that they would start to capture or break up the South African group before the night was out. He knew there were risks in making such claims, but he felt that they were calculated and reasonable risks. The President would be far from happy if Hoareau told him they had no idea at this stage what they were up against. The President in turn would not want to make such a hollow statement to the Conference.

What was wrong with a bit of optimism, Hoareau tried to

convince himself, provided the optimism had some solid basis behind it. Something would turn up from the raids. And security around the Fisherman's Cove Hotel was now so strong that the South Africans would only be able to get in with a tank. He felt entirely confident that the South Africans did not have one of those on the island and the Seychelles army had none that they could steal. Provided the delegates did nothing stupid to put themselves at risk and stayed within the conference venue, no physical harm should come to any of them - unless, as it had earlier in the night, it came from within. There is nothing I can do to protect them from each other, Hoareau thought to himself as he went up the steps of the State House.

President Baptiste willingly approved the three planned raids. Hoareau had anticipated that he would and the arrangements were already well in hand when he spoke to Baptiste. The three couples that had been singled out for close attention were Jan and Annette Gentles, Pieter and Sonia Grayling, and Henry Snell and Margot Barnard.

Jan Gentles was listed as an author on his arrival card. He was supposedly in Seychelles to write another novel They had checked and there was a South African author by that name with a number of published books to his credit. But they could not be sure that the person here using that name was in fact the real Jan Gentles. He had been in Seychelles three months but had had no contact with Seychellois officialdom that could either confirm or disprove his identity. He had been left on the list as 'not substantiated'. They had found from social security records that the Gentles employed a maid in their house at Glacis, the area to the north of Beau Vallon Bay. They found out where the maid lived and she had been surprised to receive a call from the police in the middle of the night. They had asked her a few questions about her employers, just general ones at first to try and relax her a little. Then they asked her how Mr Gentles' writing was going. She said he did not seem to do much writing as far as she could see. Most of the time when she was in the house he was either reading, writing letters, or swimming in the pool. Because of her comments, he had been left on the 'not substantiated' list when it was eventually whittled down to just three couples.

Pieter Grayling was supposedly in Seychelles to recuperate from surgery. The documentation they had did not indicate what the surgery had been for. He had been in Seychelles for six weeks. He had not had any contact with the Victoria Hospital or with the local clinic, so again they had not been able to substantiate his story. They could have checked it by contacting South African medical authorities but they decided not to do that. If Grayling was indeed an agent, any such enquiries may well only alert the South Africans.

Like the Gentles, the Graylings had a maid. That maid was also startled by a call from the police in the middle of the night. In answer to a question about Mr Grayling's health, she said he seemed quite fit. He went swimming. in the sea most days and often went walking in the hills with his wife. She did not know where they went. They often told her they were going out for a walk in the hills and would have lunch in Victoria. They did that two or three times a week. The Graylings were also left on the list as 'not substantiated'

The third couple, unlike the other two, were unmarried and made no pretence of being married. But they were more than just good friends. Henry Snell was a self-employed businessman, listed on his arrival card as a Company Director who had, so he said, decided to take six months off from the pressure of business and, in particular, to escape the present unrest in South Africa. Margot Barnard was some twenty years younger than Snell and had worked as a secretary in one of his companies. She had come on this trip as his companion/secretary. A check of South African business directories indicated that Henry Snell the businessman certainly existed. Snell and Barnard were staying in a luxurious house owned by an absentee South African owner and had been virtual recluses since their arrival three months ago. They had arrived on the same plane as the Gentles, a fact Hoareau thought may be significant. There was no reason to take them off the list.

The raids were organised to occur simultaneously at 5 am. The first light would just be paling the sky. There was less risk of the combined force of police and soldiers shooting each other or innocent bypassers if they waited until daybreak. Forty people were to be involved in each raid. They did not want to take a chance that may allow the targets to escape. All three houses were isolated, a fact that made the raids easier to organise as they did not have to worry about clearing the surrounding houses. Two of them were surrounded by bush and the third was hemmed in by rocks and the sea.

A cordon was moved into position around each house slowly and quietly well before 5 am. They were all armed but had been told that, unless there was no alternative, the 'targets' were to be taken alive. They were wanted for questioning said the briefing officer. He added as an afterthought that they may also be perfectly innocent tourists so shooting should be a last resort. At the appointed hour, small groups of armed police and soldiers were to simultaneously break down the front and back doors of the houses and quickly search them. The three raids turned out to be quite different.

At the Gentles, the couple were found still in bed, cowering under the covers wondering what the hell was going on. The scene they were in was similar to the scenes Jan Gentles wrote about in his books, which were political thrillers, but they had not expected to be participants in such a scene. They made no show of resistance other than repeated requests to be told why they were being taken in for questioning. Jan Gentles insisted continuously that all he was doing in the Seychelles was writing a book - the book wasn't even set in Seychelles, he said, thinking this may be what was concerning the authorities. The book was set in Rhodesia before it became Zimbabwe he explained so there was nothing he was writing that could concern the Seychelles government. The arresting officers tried to ignore his questions and simply repeated that things would be explained to him in Victoria. This made Gentles angry. As he got over his initial shock at having the doors of his house smashed and armed police enter his bedroom, his fear turned increasingly to anger. The suspects were all being taken to police headquarters in Victoria rather than security headquarters at the conference site. They wanted to keep them well away from the latter place. By the time Gentles and his wife were taken into Hoareau's office, Gentles' anger had the upper hand over his fear.

"I demand to know why your thugs have smashed my house,

threatened my wife and myself with guns and dragged us against our will to your police station," he shouted at Hoareau.

"Please calm yourself, Mr Gentles. Sit down and I will explain," Hoareau responded. He smiled and tried to calm Gentles by talking quietly and without threats. The threats could come later if necessary. But in his mind, Hoareau was assessing him, trying to judge if the anger was real or simulated to cover up guilt.

Gentles continued to protest volubly for a while but was finally quiet when Hoareau pointed out that he could not explain the situation to him if Gentles did not give him a chance to talk. At that Gentles subsided but continued to simmer. The anger and the fear were contained just below the surface. His wife had said nothing at all, leaving all the talking to her husband. Hoareau had intended to separate Gentles and his wife and question them individually. He had only had them brought to his office together so he could see them both and establish first impressions. He put great faith in his first impressions of people. He realized that if he tried to separate them now Gentles would explode again and that would be counter-productive. He could use the ploy of separation to unsettle Gentles later if need be.

Hoareau explained that they were investigating very serious allegations against a group of South Africans in Seychelles and they were questioning all South Africans in an attempt to identify members of the group. The all South Africans was an exaggeration but Hoareau did not want Gentles to know that he was on a very short short-list at this stage.. He said that he could not reveal the nature of the allegations but they needed to check out the legitimacy of the reasons for Gentles and his wife being in Seychelles. He was not working here, and when Gentles began to protest that of course he was working, he, was trying to write a bloody book, Hoareau quickly added that the nature of the work he was doing did not bring him into regular contact with other people. They therefore needed to check his story directly with him.

"But why check it in-' the middle of the night and why come with guns to get me? I would have come down quite willingly," Gentles interjected.

Hoareau smiled. "I am sure you understand that if your story of being an author was merely a cover then you would not be here willingly and you would not have come quietly. We could not be sure what your response would be and could take no risks. It may look like an over-reaction from your point of view, but it was necessary. You are not the only person who is receiving such an invitation tonight."

Gentles shook his head in mock disbelief. "I can show you the bloody book if that's what you want to see," he said. "The first draft is almost finished." After some more arguments and shouting from Gentles, it was agreed that it would be a good idea to see the book. It was arranged for Mrs Gentles to be driven back to their house by the police to bring the manuscript to Victoria. While she was gone, Hoareau asked Gentles about his writing habits (he did not mention what they had been told by the maid). Gentles explained that he did most of his writing in a four hour spell each day from 5.30 to 9.30 in the morning. He dictated it into a machine, his wife typed it up in the afternoon and he went over it in the evening. That explained why the maid seldom saw him writing.

Mrs Gentles arrived back forty-five minutes later with the manuscript. Hoareau skimmed through it quickly and handed it to Llewellyn, who had joined them by that time. They conferred briefly and agreed that the manuscript appeared to be genuine and probably represented the work of the last three months. They also knew by then that a thorough search of the Gentles house had turned up nothing incriminating. Hoareau hoped that the search had not inflicted too much further damage on the house or Gentles would have further cause for complaint. Gentles was brought back in and handed his manuscript. Hoareau told him that they accepted his story, they thanked him and his wife for their co-operation and apologised for any distress the investigation had _caused. They would be driven home and any damage caused to their property would be made good as soon as possible.

Gentles subsequently lodged a formal complaint with the President's office. He received a brief formal apology from President Baptiste.· The apology concluded by saying that when the South African Government failed to honour the territorial integrity of other countries and sent armed agents into those countries, their actions inevitably put all South African citizens in those countries under suspicion. The letter advised Gentles to direct his complaint to the South African Government. The Gentles decided to leave Seychelles. They had come for peace and quiet to enable him to complete his book. They had not found peace and quiet. It turned out that their experience had not been all negative. Jan Gentles had a ready-made plot which he used in his eighth book.

The second raid was, in comparison, an anti-climax, though it was the only one that produced any tangible evidence to help them identify the agents. As the police approached the front and rear doors of the house occupied by the Graylings, they startled a nightwatchman who was sleeping in an outbuilding. When the nightwatchman recovered from his shock enough to talk he told them that there was no one in the house. The Graylings had left the house the day before and had not come back last night. They had not told him where they were going but had said they would be away for three or four days. They had asked him to mind the house twenty-four hours a day until their return. The nightwatchman was usually only there at night. He had the keys to the house and reluctantly let them in. The Graylings had left him precise instructions not to let anyone in the house but he was not going to argue with the Seychelles' police.

They quickly confirmed that the house was empty. The officer in charge of the operation phoned Hoareau to explain the situation and asked what they should do next. Hoareau told him to bring the nightwatchman in for questioning and to search the house thoroughly for anything that would indicate what the Graylings were doing in Seychelles.

The poor nightwatchman was terrified but very co-operative. Yes, Mr Grayling seemed to be quite fit he said. No, he did not know what his illness was. Yes, they were out of the house quite a lot during the day and at night. Though he was only on duty there at night, he lived further down the road on which the Graylings house was and so he saw their car coming and going. Yes, they had had quite a lot of visitors lately, particularly at night. There had been four or five young men. They asked him what he meant by young. Given that the nightwatchman was probably at least sixty, anyone under fifty could have appeared young to him. No, these men were very young he said, only twenty or thirty years old. They tried to get descriptions from him but they all looked the same to him - tall, strong, white. Some had blond hair but not all of them did.

The search of the house turned up some useful things. There was a picture of a group of people and the nightwatchman subsequently identified Pieter and Sonia Grayling in the picture. He added that they looked older than that now. There was nothing in the house to indicate that Grayling was a convalescent. There were ripped up remains of an empty cartridge box in the rubbish tin in the kitchen. By the end of the night Hoareau was convinced that the Graylings were the advance party of the group of South Africans. He also thought they may be leaders of the group given that they seemed to be significantly older than the other visitors to their house. He asked for the photograph to be blown up, the images of Pieter and Sonia Grayling lifted out and enough copies made to be distributed to all police and army units on Mahe. He wanted it done as soon as possible.as it was the only solid lead they had so far.

It occurred to Hoareau later that night that he now knew what the second thing was Blake tried to tell White on Saturday - Grayling. What a pity we didn't twig that earlier thought Hoareau but until now there had been no connection.

The first raid on the Gentles had been an embarrassment. Hoareau was not unduly disturbed by that. He had known that some of the people on their short-list would prove to be legitimate visitors. The raid on the Graylings had been uneventful but useful. The third raid on the Snell/Barnard house turned out to be a debacle. The scenario was the same as for the other two raids, except that this time the house was among the rocks above the sea. The house had been surrounded quietly and efficiently and a guard put on a small runabout housed near the bottom of the steps leading from the balcony of the house to a little private beach - not legally a private beach but made private by control of the access to it.

Then the two assault groups had got into position and at a signal from the operation leader, simultaneously tried to break down the front and back doors of the house. It was not as easy as it had been at the other two houses. The hinges broke on the back door, though the lock had remained firm, and the assault group from that end of the house entered. The front door was metal-framed and proved too strong for that group. They were still outside when the next stage of the drama unfolded inside. The six men who had entered through the back door scattered and began to make their way through the house with speed, quickly searching each room they passed for a sign of the occupants. When two of the armed police forced the door of the master bedroom and entered with their guns in front of them they were met by a flurry of shots from the far side of the bed. Both fell, one dead and the other seriously wounded. The rest of the force retreated and gathered down the corridor. One of them went to let the team from the front door in but the door could not be opened from the inside without the key. So they had to go round and enter from the back also. They moved with great caution. When the full team was finally gathered the team leader shouted, "Snell, throw out your gun and come out. The house is surrounded. There is no way you can get away."

"Not likely," came back the reply, "you black bastards are not going to get your hands on me."

The operation leader was convinced that the statement tied Snell to the South African plot. There were sounds of argument from the bedroom. It appeared that the woman was trying to persuade Snell to give himself up but his replies were adamant and crude. Then they heard the sound of flesh striking flesh, a sob from the woman and the arguments stopped.

It was clear that a frontal attack on the bedroom would lead to more deaths. When they entered the bedroom they would not be able to see Snell immediately but he would be able to see them and he was obviously a good shot. People were sent outside to reconnoitre the bedroom from the outside. The curtains were drawn on the windows but the windows were open. It was too hot in Seychelles to sleep with the windows closed and Snell had obviously not had time to close them after he had become aware that the house had been broken into. There were burglar bars on the windows but there was enough space between the bars for a person to see through and for shots to be fired. One of the police crept cautiously to below one of the windows and gently raised himself to the height of the bottom of the window. He cautiously opened a small gap under the curtain. He could see Snell clearly. He was crouched behind the bed. The officer was momentarily surprised to see that Snell was nude. Snell must have slept nude and not have time to alter his condition when the attack came. A small glimpse of a leg indicated that Miss Barnard was under the bed.

The officer did not have long to study the scene. Even the small lift of the curtain had let a little more light into the bedroom and alerted Snell. He turned and fired a quick, unaimed shot at the window. The policemen hit the ground, shocked but otherwise unharmed. He scuttled back to report what he had seen. The master bedroom was at the end of a wing of the house. It had windows on both sides of the room which allowed whatever breeze there was to blow through to make the room a little cooler. This design was an advantage to the police. It was decided to get people in position under each of the windows. Those inside the house would then stage a false attack on the bedroom door, firing shots into the room to draw Snell's attention away from the windows. As soon as the groups outside heard the firing they were to pull aside the curtains and cover Snell from both sides. They had been told to take the 'targets' alive if at all possible so they would have to attempt to do that. Snell surely would not continue to fight when he saw himself so obviously trapped.

It was a reasonable plan but it did not work out the way it was planned.. Stage one went according to plan. The diversion was operated inside the house and Snell responded by returning the fire through the bedroom door. Stage two initially went according to plan. The police groups at the two windows quickly got two people into position at each window with their guns trained on the crouching figure of Snell behind his bed. They called on Snell to throw down his gun. It was at that stage that the plan went awry. Instead of throwing down his gun, Snell turned and fired at the left hand window, hitting one of the policemen there. The other police instinctively responded by firing and firing at Snell until there was no chance that he could fire back. Under the bed, Margot Barnard screamed and continued screaming long after the last shot had been fired.

When the police were eventually convinced that Snell was dead they entered the bedroom. Margo Barnard was still screaming from under the bed. She also was nude. The officer in charge, after briefly admiring her splendid body, kindly gave her the bed cover to cover herself. She took it and cowered in a corner of the room. She could not bring herself to look at Snell's shattered body and she pleaded with them not to shoot her and not to rape her. The officer tried to convince her that they did not intend to do either but she was clearly in a state of deep shock so he gave up and left her to cower in the corner. He went and phoned Hoareau who told him to have both the woman and Snell's body brought to Victoria and to himself remain and search the house thoroughly. At that stage Hoareau thought that they had eliminated one South African agent and captured another, a thought that gave him considerable satisfaction. Unfortunately it did not turn out to be that straightforward. As Margot Barnard was questioned, the real picture gradually became clear. Over the last two years Snell had become more and more obsessed with an impending black revolution in South Africa and more and more convinced that he would be murdered by the blacks unless he got them first. He was always armed. He sacked his black household staff, some of whom had been with him for over twenty years, because he no longer trusted them. Margot Barnard had been his live-in mistress for the last eighteen months. Snell's wife had died in a motor accident three years ago. The other car had been driven by a black man and Margot Barnard believed that this event had somehow unhinged Snell's sense of perspective and had been the start of his morbid fear and unbridled hatred of the blacks. He believed the accident had been no accident but a deliberate act by the blacks to eliminate his wife and that he would be their next target. Miss Barnard had become convinced that if Snell remained in South Africa he would sooner or later kill one or more blacks. In most circumstances that would not be regarded as a very serious crime in South Africa but she was afraid that Snell's obsession was gaining such a hold on him that he may kill indiscriminately. That, in the present powder keg situation in South Africa and with the eyes of the world's media on the country, could generate a scandal to which even the South African authorities could not turn a blind eye.

For months she had begged him to leave South Africa for a period and he had finally relented. He had given her four conditions on the place he was prepared to go to and left her to select the place. First, he had to be able to return to South Africa quickly by direct air connection that did not involve flying on an African airline (he did not trust any black African airline) in case his business interests ran into trouble; second, he was not prepared to go anywhere on the African continent; third, he wanted to be comfortable and hot, he was not used to and had no intention of getting used to living in a cold climate; fourth, he wanted to live in accommodation owned by a South African. He thought his four conditions were mutually exclusive and that she would not be able to find a location that satisfied all four. It had taken her a long time but then she had heard through a friend about a luxurious beach house in Seychelles owned by a vague business acquaintance of Snell's, then had found out that there was a direct British Airways flight from Seychelles to Johannesburg, and that Seychelles was fairly comfortable and definitely hot. She made arrangements to lease it for a year and Snell had agreed to come with her to the Seychelles. He had been annoyed to find so many black people in Seychelles but she managed to get him to admit that they did not have the surly, threatening appearance and demeanour of the South African blacks.

Nevertheless, he did not feel entirely comfortable in Seychelles and lived like a recluse most of the time and continued to be constantly armed. She had felt that he was becoming more relaxed over the last few weeks. But when he was awakened by intruders forcing their way into his house and armed black police had rushed into his bedroom, he had acted according to his instincts and fired in what he saw as desperate self-defence. She had tried to persuade him to give himself up but he was convinced that the black armageddon he had long believed was going to engulf him had arrived. He had died rather than surrender into their hands. It took several hours for the story to become this clear. Margot Barnard had been in a state of deep shock mixed with fear. She had no idea why Snell had.been shot and they had not enlightened her.

"What a mess," Hoareau said to Llewellyn when they finally established what had happened and why. The South African press could make quite a story out of it by putting their own slant on it. Just at that time, Seychelles or indeed the Commonwealth as a whole could do without a story about an innocent South African businessman being brutally killed by black policemen.

Hoareau decided that they did not have time to sort the matter out now. Margot Barnard would be kept in custody for the next few days for further questioning. Snell's body would be kept on ice - literally. Secretly, Hoareau hoped that they might be able to come to a deal with Miss Barnard to hush the whole thing up once she calmed down. In the meantime, he had other things to do so that would have to wait. Fortunately, as Snell had been living a fairly reclusive life no-one was likely to miss him, except Miss Barnard, and she would not be able to make a fuss, not for a few days anyway.

What a night, thought Hoareau as he had a morning cup of coffee. They had not actually got any of the South Africans in custody. The most they had achieved was to identify two of them and get a feel for how many there were altogether. He had lost two officers and they had, in turn, killed a South African visitor. He could hardly be called an innocent visitor since he had been armed, and it was illegal to own firearms in the Seychelle and he had fired first when the police had raided his house.

Yes, Hoareau concluded, they could easily justify their actions in shooting him but it would still have been better if the situation had not arisen. He would try and organise some quiet cover-up later. Right now, he had to report again to the President prior to the Conference commencing. He had snatched· only two hours sleep last night and as he contemplated the·next two days, he wondered when he would next get a decent sleep. He fought to shake off the waves of exhaustion that threatened to take control as he lay back in the back seat of the car taking him once again to the State House.

Chapter Seven

THE OPENING SESSION

The hotel was a hive of activity on Monday morning as the time for the formal opening of the Conference approached. In all forty-nine countries were attending, or forty-eight now that the Gambian delegation had decided to leave. The size of the delegations differed from just one for Brunei and Grenada to seven for Britain, Australia, India and Malaysia and eight for Canada. With authorised observers, journalists and diplomatic representatives, many of whom had come over from Nairobi especially for the occasion, the room would be jammed with around two hundred people for the formal opening.

The opening was due to commence at 10.00 but delegates had been asked to arrive at 9.30 as security checks were being conducted on everyone entering the hall. The security officers had a list of all persons authorised to attend, with pictures alongside each name to make sure that no-one got in by assuming the name of an authorised delegate. The process was slow but most- people were conscious of its necessity. Even so, some people complained about the procedures being applied 'to them', but no exceptions were made.

I arrived at 9.25 and got in with little delay as the queue was short. I was the first of the New Zealand delegation to arrive. The delegations were seated in alphabetical order which put us in the middle in direct line with the top table. We had Mauritius on our right and Nigeria on our left. The Conference room was set up in a huge rectangle with all delegations looking into the centre of the rectangle. The seats were in three rows behind the table, the number of seats each delegation had at the table depending on the delegation's size.

Most had two seats at the table but the large delegations had three. Quite clearly I would not be sitting in the front row of our delegation so I took a seat in the second row behind the New Zealand name plate and flag and surveyed the scene. This was my first such conference so it was all new and interesting to me. Many of the African and Asian delegates were again in national costume lending a cosmopolitan air to the scene. Some of the old hands at these conferences did the round of the hall as they came in, greeting their colleagues from the other delegations before taking their own seat. I felt that on the part of some of them it was an elaborate and deliberate act aimed at showing the new boys like me how well known they were in these distinguished circles. Intense conversations were being conducted in pairs or small groups all around the hall but I was happy to sit quietly on my own and observe.

As 10.00am neared, the Ministers began to arrive and the other delegates tended to break off their conversations and take up their seats near their Ministers. Gradually order was established and the arrival of the offical party was awaited. They entered soon after 10 o'clock. There was President Baptiste of Seychelles, who as Head of State of the host country would make a speech of welcome, the Hon. David Crawford, Minister of Finance for Jamaica, who would reply to the speech of welcome from the Seychelles President, and SirShridath. Ramphal, or Sonny as he was better known, Secretary- General of the Commonwealth Secretariat. He would make the opening statement and introduce the President. After the official party had taken their seats and everyone else had sat down, the Secretary-General rose again. "Honourable Presidents and Prime Ministers, distinguished Ministers, members of delegations, your excellencies, ladies and gentlemen,'· he commenced. I smiled at the formality of his opening and the length of his list,

"The Seychelles, probably more than ·any other member of the Commonwealth, dramatises the diversity of culture and race that is the distinguishing characteristic and strength of the Commonwealth. Seychelles' roots lie in Europe, on both sides of the Channel, in Africa and in Asia. These roots have intertwined to produce the Seychellois - a people that combine the features of all three cultures, and indeed, I believe they have managed to combine many of the best features of each of the three cultures," the Secretary-General said.

"Like the Seychellois, the Commonwealth is a unique blending of cultures and races. We join together not because of common race, common. geography, common economic -structure or standard of living, common political philosophy or any other common characteristic that are the raison d'etre of most other international groupings. The common characteristic that brought us together was an historical, our links with Britain. With all due respect to Britain, that is not what keeps us together now. The Commonwealth remains together because of its ability to discuss and pursue solutions to international problems within a spirit of understanding and co-operation and with a willingness to listen to each other's point of view. These are characteristics that sadly are not present in many other international forums today. Ten years ago there were many who thought that the Commonwealth would gradually become irrelevant and fade away as other international organisations became better established and more significant. Instead it has grown in size, determination and commitment. Once again at this Conference, the Commonwealth is being asked to use its ability to co-operate and display leadership of world opinion and action. The target is apartheid. The system of apartheid is an abomination. I do not think there is anyone here who would disagree with that. Apartheid is an affront to the spirit that binds this Commonwealth of nations together. The Commonwealth has in the past displayed its abhorence of that system and taken action in response. South Africa left the Commonwealth because of our views about her political system. In 1977, Commonwealth Heads of State took a momentous step when they signed the Gleneagles Agreement on sporting contact with South Africa. The unity of purpose displayed then will, I trust, serve as a precedent for this Conference. The world has no more intimate forum for dialogue that is free and frank among so representative a group of the world's Finance Ministers. It is, I am sure an occupational necessity of your high offices that you are instinctively concerned with advancing or protecting your respective national economic interests. Who better than you, therefore, to perceive that those interests should at times like this, over issues as important as this, be subsumed within the broader, international interest.'

He went on to remind delegates that though the South African issue would be dominant in their discussions, there were other matters on the Agenda that were critically important for world development and trade - the growing strength of protectionism, particularly in the industrial world, the international monetary system, the need for a further allocation of S.D.R.s, and the slowdown in aid flows to the least developed countries.

He concluded by welcoming all people there to the Conference and thanking their hosts for the warm welcome they had received, for the splendid facilities for the Conference and "for the brave and determined steps they were taking to protect the' Conference from intimidation". He did not elaborate on this latter comment. He knew it was not necessary.

After the applause that greeted his opening statement had died away, Sonny Ramphal introduced the Conference's host, the President of Seychelles. President Baptiste looked tall and thin alongside Sonny Ramphal, though he was probably only about five feet eight inches tall. He looked very stern and serious as he rose to speak.

"Your Excellency, distinguished delegates, ladies and gentlemen, it gives me great pleasure to welcome you to the Indian Ocean and to Seychelles to attend this meeting of Commonwealth Finance Ministers. Unfortunately, my pleasure is tinged with sadness and anger because your stay here has been cruelly sullied. I had intended to say that you will find Seychelles a very friendly, warm, safe and open country that extends a sincere welcome to all visitors to our shores. We rely on attracting visitors as the mainstay of our economy.

But the events of the last two days have made a mockery of those words. For the second time since independence, mercenaries from South Africa have taken advantage of our openness to try and disrupt our society and tarnish our international reputation. In 1981, their target was myself and my administration. They did not succeed in their aims. Indeed, their blatant interference and their willingness to resort to armed terrorism only served to strengthen the resolve of the Seychellois people to reassert their independence, their solidarity and their disgust with the South African regime and its system of government."

"This time their target is much wider and has a global significance. They know that this meeting is to consider the imposition of comprehensive economic sanctions against them and that it is likely to agree to impose such sanctions. They have therefore again sent mercenaries to my country to try and disrupt or divert this meeting away from taking that action against them. I pray that the result of their actions will be the same as in 1981. That far from achieving their purpose, their attack on us will strengthen the resolve of all here to act against that despicable government."

"It is my unfortunate duty," President Baptiste continued, "to report to you this morning more serious acts of aggression against this Conference from the South African mercenaries. Last night they brutally murdered our colleague and friend, the Honourable Thomas Bangura, Minister of Finance for the Gambia and one of the leading advocates of comprehensive sanctions against South Africa. We have arrested his murderer but the Gambian delegation has decided to return to the Gambia with his body. We all know what Thomas Bangura would have asked us to do when he addressed this Conference. We must not let him down; we must not let his death be in vain.'

He stopped to look slowly around the Conference hall, letting the impact of his revelations of the murder of Bangura sink in. I leant forward and whispered to Brian Franklyn, 'that's not right. The South Africans didn't murder Bangura'. "Keep quiet" Franklyn hissed and turned back to face the top table. I was surprised by the vehemence of his reaction but I noticed some of the Nigerian delegation looking at me curiosity. In their mind, their slain colleague would henceforth be regarded as another of the African martyrs in the fight against apartheid. They clearly wondered what I was arguing about.

I stole a glance around the hall during the minute's silence. Most people's heads were bowed. Some were weeping. It was a very emotional moment and it was obviously making a deep impression on most people there. While I sympathized strongly with the anti-apartheid cause, I felt like standing up and shouting 'this is a sham, he was murdered by one of his own delegation. But who would have believed me. I wondered how much Hoareau had told his President. I looked over and caught Simone's eye. She shook her head imperceptibly and quickly looked away. I vowed to talk to Brian Franklyn about it again later and, if possible, to talk to Hoareau also. But for now, the President had thanked the delegates for the tribute of silence and continued his speech.

"Last night," he said quietly, "my officers raided houses of suspected South African terrorists. One has been arrested, one was shot dead and two others identified, and we expect to arrest them shortly. The dead terrorist fired on the police who went to arrest him and, I am sad to say, he killed two of our brave and dedicated police officers before they fired back and killed him."

He again paused for effect and then raised his voice. "These desperate actions by South Africa show just how seriously that government is worried by the threat of economic sanctions. Some critics argue that such sanctions will not hurt South Africa. If that is so, why are they prepared to disrupt, terrorise and murder in order to try and prevent such sanctions being endorsed by this conference." There was silence in the hall now and most delegates looked very thoughtful. President Baptiste switched back to a quiet tone. "I feel both shame and pride for my country over the events of the last two days and those that lie ahead over the next two days. I feel shame that the integrity of my country has for the second time in our short history been attacked and sullied by that bastard regime in Pretoria. I feel shame that you have come here as our guests to our usually peaceful and friendly country and you have been forced to remain as virtual prisoners in this Conference centre because of the crude threats of their mercenaries."

"I feel pride that the police, army and people of my country are united in the attempt to identify and capture these mercenaries and have already made considerable progress in this, but at the cost of the lives of two of our loyal police. They too will be regarded by my people as martyrs to the anti- apartheid cause."

"I feel pride that the most significant step that can be taken to break the blasphemous apartheid system once and for all will be debated and decided in my country. The threats to this Conference, the threats of retribution to other countries should strengthen your resolve to isolate the government that would employ such tactics. I welcome you formally to Seychelles. I believe that this is the most significant Ministers of Finance Conference that has yet been held. The Commonwealth will make history at this Conference. I make no secret ·of what I hope that history will be - a unanimous decision to impose complete economic isolation on the racist government in Pretoria."

The President stood for a moment after he finished speaking and looked round the hall and slowly sat down. After a momentary pause, applause started up amongst the African delegates and quickly spread. The speech had been impressive in its style and very direct in its message. The gauntlet had been thrown down. The next thirty-six hours would determine whether that was the best tactic to adopt.

As the applause began to die away and the Conference waited for the next speaker I again leant forward and whispered to Brian Franklyn, "They know the murderer of Thomas Bangura wasn't a South African."

"It obviously suits them to blame the South Africans publicly to harden opinion against them. The South Africans will find it impossible to prove they didn't do it. Nobody will believe them if they deny it. All's fair in politics and war and many of the African states believe this is a war against South Africa," the Minister replied.

"But you know they didn't murder him. You aren't an African. Aren't you going to put the record straight?" I asked him. "Hell no," he responded. He looked at me as if I was a fool. Maybe I was but I had a feeling of guilt about the cover up even if no one else did. Before I could say more he told me I would be late for my phone call to New Zealand if I didn't leave before the speech of reply started.

Chapter Eight

A LONG-DISTANCE CALL

I walked toward the door of the Conference hall as unobtrusively as I could. When nobody else is moving and the place you are seated is at the furthest end of the hall from the door, it is difficult to be unobtrusive. For security reasons, only the doors at one end of the hall were being used and I was aware of the many people looking curiously at me as I made the long journey to the door. David Crawford, the Jamaican Minister of Finance was introduced by the acting-Chairman, Sonny Ramphal. He rose to reply to President Baptiste's speech of welcome as I got near the door.

I went to the security room and told them that a car and driver should have been assigned to take me to the British High Commission in Victoria. They were ready and waiting. The drive to Victoria through Beau Vallon and over the St Louis hill took just twelve minutes and was uneventful. The view of Victoria and its harbour and the off-shore islands was always spectacular as one comes down the St Louis hill. The view had looked different on each of the occasions that I had seen it, varying with the time of day, the amount of sun or cloud, which affected particularly the colour of the sea changing it from blue to green and even to black, and the amount of shipping in the harbour. For a while I was almost lost in a semi-trance, taking in the scenery, but as we entered Victoria and pulled up at the High Commission, the sight of the army guards outside the door, sub-machine gun at the ready, brought me back to the unlovely reality.

All possible targets, the major Government Ministerys, the radio and TV stations, the airport, the Central Bank and the State House were all under close guard. There was also a strong, but less obvious, security presence at all of the major hotels, partly to protect the people and partly to observe the behaviour of the tourists in the hope that some of the South Africans would reveal themselves by atypical behaviour - atypical for a tourist that is.

On entering the High Commission, I was ushered upstairs into a private office, given quick instructions on how to place my call and then left alone. I dialled the number of the Prime Minister's office in Wellington and got a quick response. "Mr White," said a female voice at the other end, some nine thousand miles away, "we were expecting your call. Just hold on while I put you through to the Prime Minister's office."

I was expecting to talk to one of the senior officials in the Prime Minister's office but to my surprise it was the Prime Minister himself who came on the line. There was no mistaking David Seddon's voice. It is a voice ideally suited for addressing large audiences and swaying them. It is deep, loud, forceful and full of expression. Even when he is not addressing a large audience but, as he was now, talking to just one person, the voice is the same. It is a voice that expects to dominate its listeners and usually does.

"Tell Franklyn that the Cabinet fully endorses the following position," he boomed. I had to hold the earpiece away from my head.

"The New Zealand government considers that South Africa has become an international terrorist rather than a law-abiding legitimate government. It has no honour left. It shows absolutely no concern about world condemnation of its actions. It is immune to diplomacy and negotiation. It has treated attempts at diplomacy and negotiation from those countries that were its friends with contempt and disdain. Its illegal control of Namibia, its raids into neighbouring, sovereign states like Botswana, and now its blatant and dangerous efforts to disrupt the Commonwealth Ministers of Finance Conference, to the extent of murdering a Minister, show that they have moved outside the bounds of tolerable behaviour in their international affairs and into the area of terrorism."

I realised that he was under the impression that the South Africans had murdered Bangura. That is what Brian Franklyn must have told him or else he had heard it on the world news. I couldn't believe that Franklyn would have deliberately lied to his Prime Minister. The thought occurred to me that I should put the matter straight but the Prime Minister was in full flight and I had to concentrate. The moment when I could have told him passed and I had remained silent.

"South Africa therefore needs to be isolated," he continued. "The time for appeasement, for bridge-building, for the so called constructive dialogue has passed. Such efforts though noble in their intention, have failed in the face of a government that has no nobility." I smiled to myself as he said this. David Seddon loved phrases like that. I could visualise him saying it. Most of his Seddonisms, as they had come to be called in New Zealand, worked well but occasionally they fell flat and made you cringe.

"Now listen carefully White," he said. I had been listening carefully all along. I realised that he was giving me large segments of Brian Franklyn's speech word for word. I hoped I could remember it all. 'The position my Government will support is this. We will support a cessation of further investment of any type in South Africa immediately. If the Conference fails to endorse that measure, we will unilaterally take that action. Second, we will support complete disinvestment over the next twenty-four months. Third, we will support the introduction of complete trade bans in twelve months time if there are no signs of meaningful change in South Africa. Have you·got that?" he asked.

"Yes," I said, "but would the goverment also be introducing the second and third measures unilaterally if the Commonwealth does not support them?"

"No," he shouted. "We are prepared to be in the forefront but we are not going to a one-man bloody army. That would be futile. Those measures will only work if everybody co-operates. Now listen. (That was to put me back in my place). The reason we are advocating the introduction of the measures in stages is to allow the South African gcvernment the chance to respond positively and avoid some of the measures. If all the sanctions were introduced simultaneously, we would drive them into a corner from where they may feel, like a rat does, that they have no option left but to fight. It could bring out the laager mentality that already exists in the Afrikaaner. Have you got that all straight?" he asked.

"Yes, sir," I responded. I quickly repeated the main points. "Right," he said. "Pass our best wishes to Brian and tell him to sock it to them. New Zealand can be seen to be taking a leading but responsible role. Tell him that I will be releasing a statement on our position on South African sanctions here in Wellington in my usual Monday evening press conference."

I smiled to myself. I hadn't thought that David Seddon would allow Brian Franklyn to get all the publicity on this issue. Seddon saw foreign affairs as his main stamping ground and he was going to get in first in New Zealand. We ended the call. I thought of making some brief notes of the main points the Prime Minister had made but as it seemed so clear in my mind and I was anxious to. get back to the Conference as soon as possible, I decided to rely on my memory.

I thanked the High Commission staff and went down the stairs to the street. The guard on duty signalled my driver, who was parked down the road, and he picked me up and we set off to return over the St Louis hill to the Fisherman's Cove Hotel. It was only 11.15.

Chapter Nine

A CLOSE CALL

As we drove back over the hill, I had time to look at the scenery. This area of the island was quite heavily populated with pockets of dense housing amongst the trees, separated by steep hills, streams and the ever present granite boulders. As we neared the LeNiol side road at the top of the St Louis hill, a car that had been stationary on the other side of the road in a bus layby suddenly started and moved towards us.

Just short of the LeNiol road it veered sideways across the road and stopped. The driver of my car turned into a side road. He shouted over his shoulder, "this is a no-exit road but we will outrun them and drive into the first big group of houses. They won't follow us in there."

I was not so confident as he was about that but I didn't argue. One thing was sure, we could not stay where we were and it would be difficult to turn around quickly and head back to Victoria. He only got as far as the first corner on the LeNiol road. As we rounded that corner, we discovered a second car was parked across the road. There was no way past. The road was quite narrow, with a high bank on the left hand side and a sharp drop on the other side. My driver stopped and started to reverse. By then the other car had come up behind us and blocked our exit. I knew my driver was armed but he wisely left his gun hidden. There were two people in each of the other cars. One person from each car quickly approached our car. One dragged my driver out, hit him hard over the head with the butt of his gun and pushed him casually over the steep drop beside the road. My pulse rate, which was already high, accelerated further when I saw their treatment of the driver but I remained where I was and tried to look calm. The other one reached in and grabbed me by the collar of my shirt. I figured that there was little point in putting up a fight. They looked so big and strong that I would have have been outnumbered in a fight if there was only one of them. Four of them, with guns as well, put the odds against me into the astronomical range. I let myself be dragged out of the car.

"You'll need to shift their bloody car," shouted one of the drivers. The voice was clearly South African. The assailant of my driver reached in and let off the hand brake of our car, turned the steering wheel and pushed the car backwards over the same bank my driver had gone over. I hoped the poor bastard wasn't in the way. The noise of the car crashing its way through the trees continued for several seconds. Everything seemed deathly quiet when the noise finally stopped.

"Come on," the other one said to me. He had a hammerlock on me so I had no choice. I was thrown into one of the cars and told to lie on the floor. Then they both climbed in, sat down and put their feet on me - heavily.

The two cars went in different directions once they left the Le Niol road. I could tell by the engine sound that we initially went up hill. That meant we were heading back towards Victoria. But it didn't take many twists and turns for me to lose my limited sense of direction. However, we drove for about fifteen minutes only so we could not have been very far from Victoria. We stopped and I was pulled out of the car again and dragged to my feet. While I had not been able to see the faces of either of the drivers, the two strong-arm men had made no attempt to hide their appearance from me. That worried me. Why did my seeing their faces not concern them? The only reason I could think of did not thrill me. Nor did they hide the house they were taking me to and that worried me some more.

"Come on," said one of them roughly, "we haven't got all bloody day," and he gave me a hard shove. I stumbled forward, hit the side of the house and fell.

"You stupid bastard," said the other, "we were told not to mark him'. They picked me up and carried me inside. I tried to figure out the significance of their comment – why should they want me unmarked. If they were going to kill me, it would not matter how marked I was. I tried to take some comfort from their comment.

I was pushed into a barely furnished room, stripped and tied to a chair. I protested at the stripping and tried to fight them but they easily undressed me without my co-operation. It is amazing how vulnerable and defensive one feels once stripped of the shell of respectability provided by one's clothes. It was hard to be dignified and determined when I felt embarrassed by my nudity in the presence of fully-clothed people. I realised after a while that there was a third person in the room. Someone was sitting in an armchair with its back to me. After the other two had finished tying me to the chair, it was the third man who spoke.

"One of you leave with the car. We shouldn't have too many of us in any one place. Even the Seychelles police might get lucky. One of you stay and help me entertain Mr White," he said in a strong Afrikaaner accent. After one of ·the others left the room, he continued. "Mr White, I apologise for bringing you here in such an undignified manner but I did not think you would accept any other invitation." I said nothing. My mouth was so dry that I was not sure that I could have said anything, even if I had wanted to.

"There were two reasons why I wanted to see you," he went on. "First, I would like to know what position New Zealand is going to take back at the conference. We know you have just been in contact with New Zealand. Second, I want you to convey a message from us back to your Minister."

He paused. At least his last statement implied that I was to be kept alive - or maybe they were going to pin the message to my dead body in order to dramatise the message. It was probably too soon to put aside my fear.

He seemed to be waiting for me to say something. I wondered how the hell he knew I had been in touch with New Zealand.

"I'm waiting for you to tell me what I want to know," he said. I was not entirely clear what he wanted me to say and my mouth still felt like a wrestler's jock-strap, so I continued to say nothing. I was not really trying to rile him but it had that effect.

"Jan, bring out the equipment and put it where Mr White can see it," he said in a cold voice. My pulse rate rose immediately. The· person behind me went to a cupboard and brought out a box from which he took what looked to me like a transformer with a number of leads running from it. I am close to completely ignorant when it comes to things mechanical or electrical so I had no idea what it was or what its purpose was. I decided not to ask. I'm usually very curious but for the second time since I had been in Seychelles, I preferred to remain in ignorance.

I decided the time had come to say something. I decided to tell him more or less the truth - not quite the whole truth and maybe not even nothing but the truth but enough of the truth to sound convincing. They would find out the truth before long anyway as the New Zealand Prime Minister was going to talk to the press in a few hours time. I did not tell him that. Neither did I tell him that New Zealand would take some of the actions unilaterally even if the Conference did not support sanctions. He didn't seem to be that interested or surprised by what I told him. He asked me no questions, either during my comments or at the end.

"Thank you, Mr White. Now it is my turn to talk and yours to listen. Please listen carefully. Your life may depend on it.' With that comment, he had my undivided attention. "The New Zealand position you have just described is not satisfactory to us. We want it to be changed." I started to say that there was nothing I could do to change it and, besides, it was now too late to change it. But he held up his hand and asked me to let him finish.

"It is probably too much to expect your Minister to turn 180 degrees and say that New Zealand opposes sanctions. We will be satisfied if he says that you are not yet ready to endorse them and want to give the matter further consideration or anything else that has the effect of delaying any decision. I am sure you are an imaginative man, Mr White and after we have given you a little demonstration of what we can do if you fail, I am sure your imagination will be enhanced. I don't care what arguments you use but you must make it clear to your Minister that we expect New Zealand to help postpone the adoption of sanctions. And I can assure you that we will know what he says to the Conference."

I could not believe what I had heard for a whole lot of reasons. For one, who did he think I was? The Minister of Finance was unlikely to change the position established by the full Cabinet of his Government on my say so, no matter what arguments I dreamed up. I tried to tell my interrogator that but he told me to shut up and listen. He had initially been very polite and relaxed but he had become much more tense and rude. Strangely enough, I had felt more threatened by him when he had been calm and collected.

He continued. 'I know what you are thinking, Mr White, your task is impossible. Well, think on this Mr White and tell your Minister this as well. If New Zealand proceeds on its proposed path, you, Mr White, will die and so will the Minister and so will your Prime Minister. We could so easily have killed you on Sunday when you tried to be a bird and fly. My men are all expert marksmen. Did you think they missed you by mistake.?' He laughed. 'We only wanted to unnerve you and your colleagues. For now, you are more valuable to us alive than dead. But only for now,' he added ominously. "If you do not succeed in doing what I have asked, your value to us will disappear. But we will not shoot at you next time. That would be too quick and easy for you. We will give you a little taste of what could happen to you next time if you fail us."

He signalled to Jan. I watched Jan set up his equipment with morbid fascination and then with mounting alarm, as I began to realise what was about to happen. But even my imagination was not sufficiently vivid and what happened was worse than I had anticipated. The transformer, or whatever it was, was plugged into an ordinary wall socket. Jan connected one of the leads to the other end of the device and approached me with the other end of the lead. It had a spring clip on it. To my complete surprise and shock he attached the clip to my penis. The clip itself hurt like hell.

'No' I shouted, and I struggled to get out of the chair. All I succeeded in doing was tipping the chair over.

"Let him lie there Jan," said the voice of the man I had never seen. "Give him just a little taste of what we can do."

As I realised what they were about to do, I began to shiver uncontrollably and I fought to stop myself from crying out. I did not want to give them that pleasure. A fragment from a poem by James K Baxter, a New Zealand poet, flitted into my mind and would not go away. Baxter was my favourite poet, in fact the only poet whose work really interested me at all. Right now I cursed him as the lines I now remembered from one of his anti-war poems were:

"The newest way," said Uncle Sam

To interrogate the brutes

Is a wet wire on the private parts that half-electrocutes

Though I do hate having to wash their vomit from my boots."

Jan went over and turned a switch on the machine. The shock was indescribable. My whole body went rigid with such sudden force that I actually propelled the chair and myself across the floor. I thought I was going to pass out - and wished that I could. Once when playing rugby I had been kicked hard in the balls. I thought I would never experience pain like that again but I was wrong. This pain was like that rugby inflicted pain only ten times worse. The pain had been so sudden and so sharp that all the air had rushed out of my lungs and all my muscles had tensed and would not untense. I could not get air back into my lungs. I couldn't breathe. I felt I was suffocating. I tried to shout but couldn't move my mouth.

After what seemed like minutes, but was probably no more than ten seconds, they turned the machine off. My penis continued to send shock waves of pain through my body but my chest muscles gradually relaxed and I was able to gasp for air. I nearly choked and vomited simultaneously but I managed to fight back the feeling of nausea. The snippet of the Baxter poem was still in my mind and I did not want to give them the satisfaction of forcing me to throw up. I could hear the South Africans laughing at my predicament. That made me even more determined but I was unsure if I would be able to withstand another shock.

"Now Mr White, we don't have much time. If we stay in one place too long, even the pathetic Seychelles police may get lucky and track us down. If you fail, we will get you. It probably won't be here in Seychelles, but sometime, somewhere, we will get to you. You won't know when and you won't know where. You will never be able to relax your vigilance again. Tell your Minister that we will get him too and he won't know where and when. If he leads the economic attack on our country we will attack back. He will be on our death list along with your Prime Minister. We still have a lot of sympathisers and some influential friends in the world. The sanctions will rebound against you and your country. We will do more harm to your country than you will do to ours. The French have shown how easy it is for foreign agents to infiltrate your petty little country. Our agents will be much more efficient and much more deadly than those bungling French ones. We can wreck your tourism industry by spreading fear - one or two bombs strategically placed plus the threat of more will soon drive tourists away from New Zealand. We can easily destroy your agriculture by introducing diseases. You tell your Minister that if you start an economic war against us, we will start one against you. The difference is that we will carry it through until we have destroyed your government. Your government will lose its nerve long before ours does. Tell him all that. I am sure he will see where his personal and your country's national interests lie. We are not asking New Zealand to be a turncoat. You can keep your national dignity. You just need to delay taking a position. That is all we are asking of you. It is not a great deal given what is at stake. Our little demonstration now was to convince you that we are serious and to motivate you for your role as messenger. We will leave you now. The police will be here shortly to rescue you. We need you to get back to your Minister quickly to deliver our message. Remember we will be watching you. We will be aware of all you say and do."

With that he walked to the door, still keeping his back to me. Jan followed with the box of equipment. I heard a car drive away. The only thing they had left on my body was my watch. I glanced at it. To my amazement it was only 12.30. Only just over an hour had elapsed since I left the British High Commission. I struggled to raise myself and the chair but I didn't have the leverage or the strength so I quickly gave up. I glanced furtively at my penis. It looked remarkably unaffected by its shocking experience but it still throbbed uncomfortably.

I was at a loss what to do next. I knew I would have to make some effort to draw attention to myself. There must be people quite close to the house I was in. We had only driven for fifteen minutes, initially going towards Victoria so we could not be far out of Victoria, and most of that are was densely populated. I gave a yell for help. It was half-hearted. The truth was I felt embarrassed. Whoever came would find me tied to a chair and nude. I realised that I had no alternative. I could not cower there for ever. I could not even cower there for long as I had to get back to the Conference to report on my call to the Prime Minister and to pass on. the South Africans' warning. I also had a strong desire to get out of that house in case the South Africans came back. Even though my rational mind told me that was unlikely, the irrational part of my mind screamed at me to get away from there. So I tried again. This time the shout was louder. I got an instant response. I heard the sounds of running feet and three policemen, including Inspector Hoareau pushed carefully into the room. They looked cautiously around the room, satisfying themselves that there was no one else there besides myself.

"Get me out of this bloody chair," I yelled at them. Hoareau looked at me and then laughed. The other two policemen joined in the laughter. I did not find the situation at all amusing and was furious with them.

"You may be enjoying yourselves but I'm not. Get me out of this bloody chair now," I shouted. One of the men finally untied me and I struggled to my feet. I recovered my clothes from where they had been strewn across the floor and struggled into them, thus establishing a bit of dignity.

"How did you respond to my shout so quickly?" I asked Hoareau when I was dressed and a little calmer.

"We were already in the house," said Hoareau. "An anonymous phone call to one of our stations had tipped us off as to where you were. We had realised you were missing as your car and driver had been located. We were easing our way slowly into the house in case it was a trap when we heard your yell." I told him I needed to get back to the Conference as soon as possible as I had important matters to report to my Minister. He asked me if I was injured. Only my pride and my penis I replied and, in response to his look of surprise, I said I would explain in the car.

He told me that the police driver was alive but in hospital in a serious condition. As well as the initial injuries he had received when hit on the head and pushed over the bank, the car had run over him when it ran down the bank and he had a skull fracture, broken ribs, and internal injuries. As we drove back to the Fisherman's Cove Hotel I quickly ran over what had happened to me. I said nothing about the threats that had been made to me or the Minister and only alluded briefly to those made against the country. I felt I knew what Brian Franklyn's response would be but I wanted to be sure first.

I gave Hoareau a description of Jan, assuming that was his real name, and the other assailant. Hoareau said he would talk to me again after I had spoken to my Minister and try to get me to expand the descriptions. I was not sure that I would be able to add much.

"What about the one who questioned you?" asked Hoareau. 'He seemed to be the leader."

"He was careful to make sure that I did not see him clearly," I responded. "He was certainly older than the others. I'd say he was around fifty. He had fairish hair, cut very short, and he was quite tall. Not as tall as Jan but probably around six feet. He had a strong Afrikaaner accent."

"So there were five people in all involved in your abduction. Four of them were in their twenties and one much older. Did they mention any others in their discussion with you?" Hoareau asked. I replied that they had not.

"We believe there is a woman as well so that makes at least six. I think I know who your questioner was. Your description of him, even though limited, matches the description we had from another source. We should be able to pick him up before too long," Hoareau told me. I was pleased. I certainly did not want to see him again. I had to admit, the personal threat he had made had me worried. I didn't fancy continually looking over my shoulder or under my bed for the next several years, and much less did I fancy being dead.

We arrrived back at the Conference Centre at about 1.30pm. I assured Hoareau I was okay, which was a bit of an exaggeration, and arranged to meet him later. I went to find Brian Franklyn. The morning session of the Conference had finished at 1.00· so I assumed he would be in the dining room. The afternoon session started at 3.00 and he was due to speak soon after the restart.

Chapter Ten

THE MINISTER'S ADDRESS

I looked around the dining room and saw that Brian Franklyn was dining with the rest of the New Zealand delegation at a separate table in a corner of the room. They all looked at me like, I presume, judges would look at a man they were about to sentence to hang by his neck until dead. I started to offer an apology and explanation but the Minister got in first.

"Sit down," he growled, indicating a chair across from him at the table, "Where the hell have you been?" Before I could answer he went on. "I told you to phone David Seddon, not go all the bloody way to Wellington to visit him. John Kershaw sniggered but ·was silenced by a glare from the Minister. The Minister was not joking. He was very angry.

I briefly explained what had happened to me. His anger gradually dissolved as I spoke and he shook his head in disbelief. "Christ, you have a nose for trouble," he said. It wasn't my nose that got into trouble this time I thought. I had not gone into details of the method of torture they had used or the part of my anatomy it had been directed against. Having got their attention, I then passed on the main details of the threats against the country and against Franklyn and Seddon. I had not mentioned the threats to myself.

Brian Franklyn thought we should ignore the threats to persons. They were only trying to scare him and, even if they were serious, he could not allow it to change New Zealand's position. The others all agreed, though as their skins weren't at stake, agreement was easy.

In the face of his readiness to ignore the threats to himself, I could hardly argue for a reconsideration of the position on the basis of the threat to myself so I said nothing and tried to dismiss the threat from my mind. The threats to the country were more serious. There was little doubt that the South Africans would have the capacity to carry out the threat against the tourism industry and probably the threat against agriculture as well, though New Zealand's vigilance in the area of agricultural diseases was fairly sharp and any outbreak that the South Africans could initiate could, hopefully, be quickly contained. There was little doubt that the threats, if carried out, would have a severe impact on the New Zealand economy. The economy was dependent on trade and the current account was already in deficit and had been so continuously for over a decade. The level of external debt was high so the country was not in a strong position to withstand a major setback to any of its main foreign exchange earning sectors. But Brian Franklyn thought that these threats should also be ignored for now. They could be dealt with later should anything concrete eventuate. He decided that he would not convey them to the Prime Minister until after his address. Sharp started to argue that the Prime Minister should be told in case he saw things differently but Franklyn bluntly told him no.

The Minister asked me to go ever what David Seddon had said. I went through it in some detail and he was delighted. "Let's go and write that up," he said.

"I haven't had lunch," I pointed out. There were three others in the delegation I thought. Why couldn't one of them write it up. None of them made an offer to assist. After what I had just been through I felt I deserved a little sympathy and consideration. Besides, I had missed out on breakfast also in order to do more work on his address. That's what I thought but I didn't say it.

"If you insist on being late all the time, you'll have to go without," Brian Franklyn said. This time he did say it jokingly but he also meant it. He rose from his chair and walked off. I had no choice but to follow.

I remembered the Prime Minister's comments virtually word for word, including the better Seddonisms, and we drafted them into the speech unabridged. Brian Franklyn seemed to have forgotten the threats altogether and was looking forward to the afternoon session. I could not forget the threats so easily. He left after a while and I had to type the new sections of his speech out with my three finger style as there was not time to use the Conference secretarial services and we did not have a secretary with our delegation. At least his departure gave me the opportunity to call room service and order two sandwiches and coffee to ward off my hunger. I got the typing and my sandwiches finished just in time for the beginning of the afternoon session.

After a few housekeeping formalities had been dealt with, the Conference Chairman, President Baptiste, called Brian Franklyn as the first speaker after lunch. He rose and walked to the podium. As all the other speakers had done, he opened with thanks to the hosts for their hospitality, thanked the Commonwealth Secretary General and his staff for the highly relevant documentation for the Conference and congratulated Baptiste on his unanimous election as Chairman of the Conference. The host country Minister of Finance was always elected Chairman but every speaker still solemnly congratulated him on the appointment nevertheless. President Baptiste was also Minister of Finance. He had said on accepting appointment as Chairman that "few persons who have not lived and worked in a small society are able to realise the extent of social compression that occurs. We must all wear more than one hat. I have already welcomed you as President I now accept the honour of chairing this meeting as Minister of Finance. In another capacity, as Minister in Charge of Security Forces, I am responsible also for your personal welfare, security and protection." He had then used this as a lead to talk again about the 'South African outrages."

Brian Franklyn had now finished the preamble to his address and was setting the scene for disclosing the New Zealand position.

"Over the last decade, the divisions between the rich and poor countries, between developed and developing countries, between the so-called North and the South,- have got deeper and sharper. There has been more talk about these issues in this decade than ever before. International conferences have been one of the world's few growth industries. All that talk has led to distressingly little positive action however. Though they are talking, the two groups do not seem to be listening to each other. Where they are listening, they are failing to understand each other's position. On all sorts of issues the North and the South have moved further away from rather than closer to solutions. That saddens me. New Zealand feels it can understand both points of view. We are generally regarded as a member of the North grouping even though in geographic terms if we were much further south we would be part of Antarctica'. There was some polite laughter but the mood of the Conference was too serious to react to light relief.

"New Zealand is a member of the OECD, disparagingly referred to as the rich man's club by the developing countries. However, we have found ourselves over the last several years in the major international forums such as the IMF Board and the United Nations General Assembly, often supporting the positions advocated by the South or adopting a middle ground, rather than supporting the positions advocated by the major northern powers."

"There are a number of reasons why New Zealand has come to take up such a position in international affairs. It is partly because of our small size. This had led us, at times, to see the North's position as paternalistic - generally well-meant but unjustifiable. It is partly because of our traditional dependence on the export of primary products, which means that we have for a long time, out of self-interest, shared many of the concerns of the developing countries at the unfair trading practices carried on in many industrial countries. It is partly because of the multi-racial nature of our society. That has taught us to tolerate and try to understand the viewpoints of others. It is partly because of our geographic isolation in the South Pacific. This, we believe, allows us to take a more detached view of international issues than most other countries can afford."

He went on to repeat the comments that David Seddon had made about South Africa becoming nothing more or less than an international terrorist. He then went through the actions that the present government in New Zealand had already taken to express their antagonism to apartheid. They had let it be known that they would close the South African Embassy in Wellington. The South Africans had taken that hint and withdrawn their ambassador before the New Zealand government expelled him. They had vigorously opposed an All Blacks rugby tour of South Africa.

"Our opposition to the tour was an important element in creating the climate of opinion in New Zealand which led a court to issue an injunction against the tour on the grounds that the tour was not in the best interests of New Zealand rugby," he continued.

"We are now prepared to go further in order to put pressure on the South African government." He went on to set out the New Zealand position as advised by the Prime Minister: they would support the immediate adoption by the Commonwealth of the cessation of further investment of any type in South Africa. If the Commonwealth did not endorse this, New Zealand would take the action unilaterally; they would support complete disinvestment over the next two years; they would support the introduction of complete trade bans in twelve months' time if there were no signs of meaningful change in South Africa.

I thought it was quite a neat compromise position. It promised the hard-line states something immediately and all they wanted in time. By delaying the toughest sanctions and making their introduction conditional upon no progress in South Africa, it gave those members who wanted to continue to try and talk the South Africans into change, one last chance. I glanced around the hall. Most of the African and Caribbean delegates looked quite pleased. The Australian and Canadian delegations looked thoughtful. The British delegation looked sour - as usual. Most of the Asian delegations looked enigmatic - as usual.

I returned my attention to the Minister. He was winding up his address. He sat down to genuine and prolonged applause from most of the delegates. The Nigerian Minister leaned over and shook his hand warmly. Brian Franklyn looked as pleased as punch. He leant back and whispered to me, "Maybe the left wing of the party will love me after this." I smiled. The Minister's economic policies in New Zealand tended to be orthodox and market based. As a consequence, he had a constant battle with the left wing of the Party on economic issues. That left wing felt very strongly about the South African issue so for once the Minister of Finance had been cast in the role of their champion.

The rest of the afternoon was predictable. There were speeches from the Ministers from Ghana, Solomon Islands, and Tanzania. They all commended New Zealand on its position but thought that the Commonwealth should act now, not in a year's time. South Africa had received many previous warnings and they could see no case for giving them yet another one. The Canadians and British were not scheduled to speak until the second and final day of the Conference and everyone was waiting anxiously to see if they would support the New Zealand position. A formal resolution, if one was to be put, would not be moved and voted on until the last session on Tuesday afternoon. It was not certain that a formal resolution would be put. If there was a lack of consensus, the debate would probably be left unresolved and member governments asked to consider taking their own actions. This, though weak, would be regarded as preferable to the indignity and political embarrassment of an open argument and split. Indeed, a resolution that did not have unanimous support had little status. If forty-six countries voted for some form of action and three opposed, the adoption of the resolution would have no formal or legal standing as far as requiring action from the three was concerned. So intense lobbying would go on before the final session to try and get a resolution worded in a way that would get unanimous support. Even then, the decision of this Conference would not be legally binding on any of the Commonwealth governments, but it would have strong moral force. It would also be intensely embarrassing politically for any Minister of Finance who gave his government's support for action at this meeting to have his government subsequently refuse to act. So despite the lack of legal power, the decision of this Conference was being treated by all here as the crunch decision. The South Africans obviously viewed it in the same light.

Now that Australia and New Zealand had stated positions supporting some form of economic sanctions, the lobbying pressure would fall upon the Canadians and the British. It was unlikely that anyone else would hold out against the overwhelming support of the other Commonwealth members, except probably for Malawi, but everyone else ignored them. If Canada was persuaded to support sanctions, the British, who had previously stated consistently that they were opposed to their introduction, would be in an isolated and awkward position. The Commonwealth was no longer taking their lead from Mother England but were ganging up to push her to adopt their point of view.

Chapter Eleven

WORDS AND MORE WORDS

The Canadian and New Zealand delegations dined together that evening. Brian Franklyn was trying to persuade the Canadian Minister, Frank Clark, to support the New Zealand position or, failing that, at least support some form of clear positive action. Franklyn pointed out that the South Africans would regard it as a great propaganda victory if the Conference was unable to reach an agreed position and postponed the issue. Clark accepted that but would still not commit himself. He said he still had doubts about the morality and effectiveness of the use of trade sanctions as tools of political change. It would mean asking some of their own Canadian citizens, those who owned assets in South Africa or traded with South Africa, to pay a personal price to put pressure on a foreign government. Normally, Canada would not even contemplate such a policy. Canadian citizens would not stand for it. He felt was being pushed into doing something that was against their own better judgement by the weight of opinion from other countries.

Brian Franklyn asked if there would be widespread criticism and a political backlash in Canada if they supported sanctions. Frank Clark had to admit that there probably would not. Public opinion was heavily against the South African regime and those who would normally object to such an infringement of the individual's right to trade with whom they liked may well keep quiet for fear of being labelled a supporter of apartheid.

"The whole issue is a mess, a nightmare of conflicting points of view," said Frank Clark. "There is no middle ground left. If you are not prepared to oppose apartheid you are labelled a supporter of it. I cannot see where it all ends and that worries me. What sort of a precedent would we be creating. I am sure the precedent the Commonwealth would create by imposing sanctions on South Africa will come back to haunt us later."

I thought to myself that the precedent had already been well and truly created. The British had done it with Rhodesia. The Americans had done it with Cuba and now with Nicaragua. In fact, I was aware of a recent study by the Institute of International Economics in Britain that had instanced 108 cases where economic sanctions had been used for political purposes since 1914

The dinner broke up at that point. The Ministers said they wished to talk in private. I managed to catch Brian Franklyn's attention before he left and I told him that the precedent of using trade sanctions for political ends had already been set and gave him some of the major examples. Frank Clark could forget about his concern for establishing precedents. That concern was many years too late. What the Canadians needed to decide was whether this particular political objective justified the use of this means. The Minister said he would put that to Frank Clark and see what his response was.

I found myself at the bar with Simone Lablache, John Kershaw, another Canadian, Phil Daube, and three Kenyan delegates, Eliphaz Ruheni, Francis Omani, and Robert Wamalwa. The two Canadians seemed as uncertain about the position their Minister would take as the rest of us. Either they were being very diplomatic or they were genuinely in the dark. I thought the latter. We speculated about what the South Africans would do next to try and disrupt the Conference. None of them, except John Kershaw, knew of my kidnap that morning and the threats that had been made against New Zealand. I did not think that our Minister had passed that on to anyone and I had only told Inspector Hoareau half the story. My interview with Hoareau and Llewellyn earlier that afternoon had not gone well. I had tried hard to remember details of the two South Africans I had seen but my description had remained very vague and general. Llewellyn, in particular, had been scathingly critical.

"Half the male tourists on the island would fit your description," he said. "Think, man, think. Don't you realise how important this is. Given what they were doing to you, you can't possibly have been that unobservant about them."

I had a very good memory for faces and I knew that I would

certainly recognise those two if I saw them again. Their faces were etched clearly in my mind. That was not the problem. The problem was that I could not convert the image in my mind into a verbal description. I had had no experience of doing so and could not get much beyond generalities like fair hair, blue eyes, tall, solidly built. Irritated by Llewellyn's rudeness, I decided to question them in turn.

"How is it," I asked, "that the President announced to the conference that the Gambian Minister was killed by the South Africans? You know that isn't true."

Both Hoareau and Llewellyn had looked at me as if they would like to squash me like a cockroach. But Hoareau answered my question reasonably politely. "It was announced that way in order to make delegates more conscious of the seriousness of the security risks and also to help solidify opinion against South Africa," he said.

"But it is a lie," I repeated doggedly. Hoareau then lost his cool. "Don't be so stupid and naive," he said loudly. "This isn't a game. We aren't playing cricket," he added sarcastically. "This is deadly serious. They will stop at nothing to achieve their aims. We have to be just as single minded and determined."

I found it hard to accept Hoareau's philosophy. It implied that if you faced a ruthless, dishonest opponent, then you had to be just as ruthless and dishonest to beat them. I wanted to argue about that idea but, seeing the looks on Hoareau's and Llewellyn's faces, I decided to let it ride.

I prepared to leave, but Llewellyn decided he was not ready to let the issue ride.

"White," he said as I neared the door. "What's happening is deadly serious'. He managed to make the word deadly very sinister and threatening.

'If the information that Bangura's murder was an inside job gets out, we will have a lot of difficulty maintaining security at this Conference. Everybody will ease their watchfulness and the South Africans are sufficiently professional to take full advantage of any such slip up. If the information gets out, we will know where it has come from. I will hold you personally responsible. You will not have to worry only about the South African threats to you, you will need to worry about me also. I don't like you Mr. White. You are a weak link in our security arrangements. I would get considerable personal satisfaction from taking you out."

I looked at him in amazement. Was his last comment a death threat? That's what it sounded like to me but I couldn't believe it could be so. Maybe the phrase meant something less than that. The look on his face, however, dissuaded me from asking him to clarify what he meant. I looked towards Hoareau, but he looked away and would not catch my eye.

I stared back at Llewellyn for a while but then turned and left the room without saying anything. Some of the group at the bar thought that there was now little the South Africans could do to alter the outcome. Indeed, they argued, if South Africa made more attempts at disruption, it could work against their objective by hardening opinion against them. Others disagreed. Eliphaz Ruheni said that if they were prepared to go as far as murdering right here in the hotel, they would stoop to anything. He then looked at me and said, "If I was your Minister I would sleep very lightly tonight."

I had a moment of alarm on Brian Franklyn's behalf. Then I remembered that it was not the South Africans who murdered Thomas Bangura. I was about to say so when I realised that Eliphaz and most of the others did not know that and anything I said would contradict the official version of what had happened. Llewellyn's threat came back to me clearly and strongly so I kept quiet. John Kershaw began to say "Thomas Bangura wasn't" when I kicked him sharply under the table. His initial reaction was anger and I thought he was about to punch me. At least it had stopped him talking. Then it dawned on him what he had nearly blurted out and he subsided a little. The others looked on with some amazement at this exchange between us. I tried to console myself that we were not lying. We were just not allowing the truth to be known. Somehow it seemed a rather spurious distinction.

John Kershaw had clearly been thinking of a way to recover his dignity with the group and get back at me. He started to tell them about the threats that had already been made to New Zealand. I caught his eye - I thought I had better not press my luck and kick him again - and shook my head. I thought he would have enough sense to take the hint but he ignored me and carried on. He was enjoying having the full attention of the others. He always liked being the centre of attention and I think he felt that I had been hogging the limelight within our delegation up until now. I certainly had not been seeking it and I would have gladly changed places with him on some of the occasions. He was trying particularly hard to get Simone's undivided attention but though she was listening to him with interest, she kept looking over at me, much to his annoyance. He began to get very specific about the nature of the threats.

As he would not take the hint, I decided I had to be direct. "John, the Minister did not want this made public," I said. He looked at me with scorn, "Why not?" he asked. I realised he was baiting me. He knew the answer as well as I did but he hoped to embarrass me. It was his style. He had made his progress up the Treasury ranks more by belittling his competition than by any outstanding work performance of his own. He played the role of critic of others work very well and he was careful not to commit himself to views or to write anything on his own that could open him up for similar criticism. Frankly, I found him a pain in the neck but the last thing I wanted to do now was to play word games with him. So all I said was "you know as well as I do" and I walked away from the group to a seat at the other end of the bar. I heard Kershaw's horsey laughter following me.

My black mood lifted a few minutes later when Simone also left the group and joined me at my end of the bar.

"You don't like him very much do you?" she said as she sat down. "Is it that obvious?" I replied. She nodded. "What did he say after I left?' I asked.

"He really said little more about the threats but he made some disparaging remarks about you. He said it was you rather than the Minister that wanted nothing said as you were the one who conveyed the message from the South Africans and you were running scared. Then he said that he had better respect your wishes and not say any more," she said. The bastard generally managed to get the last word in, that was what was so frustrating about him.

South Africa's next attempt at disruption occurred that night but came from 2000 miles away. It had, from their point of view, a more favourable impact on opinion than point of view, a more favourable' impact on opinion than anythi g they had done so far in the Seychelles.

That evening, news stories broke across the world that tribal factions were involved in bloody fighting in the remote northern provinces of Kano and Katsine in northern Nigeria, and the fighting had spread across the border into Niger. The news items said that the situation was very confused but it seemed that the conflicts were not political in nature. All remained calm in the capital of Lagos. It seemed to be simply a violent outburst of long-standing tribal antagonisms. Deaths were very high and many of the deaths had been very brutal. It was thought that total deaths were already over one thousand and rising. Many of the dead were women and children as it was said that anyone who was caught in the wrong tribal area was being slaughtered indiscriminately. In many circumstances the story, being vague and remote, would have got little media attention. But because the eyes of the world's media were focussed on Africa at that moment because of the Commonwealth's debate on economic sanctions, it got considerable attention, with some help from an extensive and well-oiled pro-South African propaganda network.

The story spread around the Conference delegates like wild-fire. The journalists present had not been able to attend the sessions after the formal opening. They had found it difficult to get anybody to talk about what had happened in the Conference sessions, even off the record, as nobody wanted to prejudice or prejudge what might happen. So these journalists, in the position of having to file some story from the conference each day to justify their all-expenses paid sojourns in Seychelles, seized on the Nigerian story as a lead into reactions here.

They button-holed as many Ministers as they could, told them what the story from Nigeria was and asked for their reaction on how it might affect the African debate at this Conference. They got little reaction but enough for them to file stories around the world. Before long, everybody at the Conference knew and was talking about the story.

The story was also quickly editorialised by the British press with all the major dailies had editorials on it the next morning. While most of us were not aware of this until later, the UK delegation were informed via their High Commissionas soon as it became obvious that the story had struck a strong emotional chord in the UK press. Most of the editorial comment was spontaneous and well intentioned. Some of it, however, was the result of the prompting of the editorial conscience by some conscience money being judiciously applied by South African sympathisers. That was also known only much later.

The general editorial line was that "this fighting was symptomatic of the core problem of African self- determination. Tribalism and nationalism were frequently inconsistent forces and tribalism was much the stronger emotion of the two as 'The Observer' put it. Most editors left it at that but those whose eyes had been opened by the priming of their pockets added something like "similar tribal problems are likely to arise in South Africa if the one-man, one vote system of government was introduced there. Those advocating radical change in South Africa were ignoring what had happened in most of the rest of that blood-covered continent was how the News of the World put it.

It was not until a week later that the realization began to dawn on the Western press that the story had been a classic piece of disinformation - a deliberately created fabrication. The two or three enterprising journalists who had made the difficult journey into the remote 'war-zone' to get first-hand information and write follow up stories could find nothing untoward. The areas were outwardly and inwardly calm. For some reason, stories that no tribal violence seemed to have occurred in the Kano and Katsina provinces of Nigeria after all were not regarded as front page news by the Western press. In fact, they were not regarded as news at all. The story simply faded out of sight and largely out-of-mind.

The Nigerian Minister of Finance sought leave of the Conference to make a statement at the beginning of the following morning's session. He said that he had contacted his authorities. They vehemently denied that there was any tribal fighting in his country.

"The story is false; it is a malicious lie," he had shouted, "spread by the enemies of my country."

The other delegates had looked knowingly at each other. Some of them wondered if that Minister would be at next year's conference, or in exile; or dead. For all of them believed that where there was smoke, there must be fire, and all of them believed that the news story implied there was some smoke in Nigeria. It never occurred to them that the Minister may be telling the truth.

From the point of view of the South Africans, it did not matter if it was discovered later that the story was a complete fabrication. It had served its purpose. The story had given the British, and the Canadians if they wanted it, another argument to use against the imposition of sanctions and it had weakened the position of the Nigerian delegation. As the largest country in black Africa, they played an important role in leading and articulating African opinion. The pen, particularly the poisoned pen, is frequently mightier than the knife or the gun. An initial statement or accusation was generally treated as hard news. The inevitable denial was usually printed but in a ho-hum fashion - of course they would deny it was the general attitude of both editors and readers. Very seldom were stories followed up to find the truth. And if they were, and it turned out that the press had been misled or duped by the initial story, they preferred not to admit it. If only one paper or television channel had run with the story in the beginning then the rest would take malicious delight in letting the world know how their competitor had been tricked or had misled the public and maligned some poor person or country. But if they had all been taken in by the initial story, as has happened in this case, there was a conspiracy of silence. They knew they were all in that particular glass house together so no one threw the first stone.

Chapter Twelve

HOAREAU RUNS HOT AND COLD

The South African's second attempt that evening to influence the Conference was based on the pen as well, but this one involved an open threat of action and was much closer to the Conference itself. A Seychellois taxi driver had arrived at the Conference centre at 8.30 pm with three letters he had been asked to deliver to the Fisherman's Cove Hotel. They were addressed personally to Samuel Linchwe, Minister of Finance for Botswana Tibus Banda, Minister of Finance for Lesotho, and Julius Fundafunda, Minister of Finance for Swaziland.

The taxi driver was questioned closely but there was little useful he could tell the police. A woman had approached him at the taxi stand between Barclays Bank and the Courthouse in Victoria and had asked him to deliver the letters to the hotel She had paid him well and he had not asked her anything else. He could not really describe her. It had been dark. She had leaned in the passenger side window of his car, put the letters on the seat and then stood up outside the car and spoke to him. He had seen her face again when she leant down to pay him but he had to admit that he had looked more closely at the money than at the woman. She had not been very beautiful so she had not held his attention. All he could say was that she was white, skinny and middle-aged. Such women all looked the same to him he said. He could not say what colour her eyes were or what colour her hair was or what she was wearing. Despite the skimpiness of his description, Hoareau was quite sure the woman was Sonia Grayling.

.They thanked the driver for his assistance, told him to tell his fellow drivers to take careful note of the people involved if they got similar requests to deliver anything to the conference, though Hoareau thought it very unlikely that the South Africans would use the same procedure again, and let him go.

The letters were taken to the security room. One of the local officers said, jokingly, that they could be letter bombs and, to his surprise, Hoareau agreed with him. It was decided to treat them with caution. Representatives of the three delegations were summoned, told how the letters had arrived, and advised by Hoareau that there was a possibility that one or more of the letters could be a letter-bomb. Though the·letters were addressed to their Ministers and marked as confidential, the Seychelles police were responsible for the safety of those Ministers while they were in Seychelles and they therefore intended to open the letters Hoareau said. They would endeavour to do so in a way that did not destroy the contents but that could not be guaranteed. He asked the delegation representatives if they had any objection to that proposal. None of them did. They each knew that if they did object and delivered the letter to their Minister, they would have to open it. Hoareau's nervousness about the letters had got through to them so that the idea of being the one to open the letters held no appeal whatsoever. They were all convinced that the letters were letter bombs, or that, more likely, one of them was and the other two were decoys. None of the delegates fancied playing that particular version of Russian roulette.

"How do we get them open?" asked one of the police on duty in the security room.

"Come with me and I will tell you," Hoareau replied. He asked the three delegates to wait where they were.

"There is no point in you risking your lives as well as us, though you are welcome to come and observe if you so wish," Hoareau said to them. None of them wished to. They said they had complete trust in the Seychelles police. Hoareau smiled. He knew damn well that that was not the reason why they had no wish to observe the opening of the letters. Despite his cynicism, Hoareau was relieved. The truth was that he had no idea at that stage how to open the letters safely. They did not have the necessary sophisticated equipment in Seychelles, let alone at this hotel but he did not want to reveal that to the foreign delegates.

The police went into the back room and the other officers looked expectantly at Hoareau. He put the letters on a desk and slowly turned to face the other three officers in the room.

"Well, who can tell me how to open them without blowing ourselves to bits?" he asked. Nobody replied. The other officers all tried to avoid catching Hoareau's eye. None of them had had any experience with letter bombs, real or suspected. They were unknown in the Seychelles. They had only read about them. Letter bombs seemed to a peculiarly English, or more often Irish device.

Where the hell was Llewellyn when we need him thought Hoareau. He was always around being a bloody nuisance when Hoareau could do without him Now that Hoareau could do with his advice, he wasn't there. Hoareau knew that Llewellyn was probably catching up on sleep in his room. None of them had had much sleep over the last forty eight hours. He thought there would be a certain satisfaction in waking Llewellyn. But Hoareau was also aware that Llewellyn regarded himself and his British team as indispensable to the security operations for the Conference. Llewellyn did not believe that the Seychellois could handle any aspect of it without his guidance, advice and direction. Hoareau could not stand Llewellyn's arrogance so he allowed his pride to overrule his judgement and he left Llewellyn sleeping. He will wake up soon enough if one of these things is a letter bomb he thought wryly to himself.

"There are two approaches we can take," Hoareau finally said to the others. "We can try and build up a safety wall of some sort - heavy metal I presume would be necessary - place the letters behind the wall and have a person with some heavy-duty safety device on his arm, put his arm around the wall and open the letters." Hoareau was thinking aloud. Even as he spoke, he knew that the idea was impracticable. It was possible to pack a lot of explosive power into a small area so he thought that it may be difficult to rig up a wall that would be strong enough to withstand the blast.

But that was not the main problem with the idea. He had built up the scene in his mind's eye and realised it would be almost impossible to open an envelope with one hand only. If the letter was. anchored in some way it may just be possible but in anchoring the letter securely they were likely to set the damn thing off anyway. If the person had to use both hands, then most of his body would need to be exposed, unless he was a contortionist, and they did not have the equipment to rig out a whole body in protective clothing.

He had been silent, thinking, for some time.

"What is the second approach, Sir?" one of the officers finally asked. Hoareau looked at him carefully, wondering if he was trying to be smart. He decided not.

"Everybody leaves the area except one person who volunteers to take the risk and simply opens the letters in the normal manner," he said. He continued quickly before any of them could raise objections. "There are no outward signs indicating that they are letter bombs. They are all the same weight and thickness as far as I can tell. I very much doubt that all three of them could be letter bombs so hopefully these similarities mean that none of them are and we are being over- sensitive."

He paused and then he said, "Is there a volunteer? He had not expected any. But to his surprise, the youngest of the three officers said he would do it if that was what the Inspector wanted. The other two officers looked at him in amazement. Hoareau looked at him with pride, though inwardly he cursed him a little. Constable Pilley was young, keen and idealistic. He sincerely believed in all those ideas like loyalty to the state and duty towards your country and your countrymen that the Seychelles National Youth Service had brow beaten into him in his two year period in the NYS when he was fourteen and fifteen. Hoareau reflected briefly on this change of attitude. He knew that when he was younger, he would never have offered to stick his neck out in the way that Pillay had.

But Hoareau, though he did not realise or admit it, was equally bound by a set of values that included loyalty and duty, though he tended to think of it in terms of the loyalty and duty he owed to himself and the police force, rather than to the more intangible concepts of state or country. The end result as far as appropriate action was concerned was often the same however. Hoareau knew he could not accept Pillay's offer. His sense of duty as the senior officer did not allow him to put a subordinate's life in danger if he was not prepared to face the risk himself. Because of his sense of pride, he knew that he could not now dismiss the idea of someone opening the letters directly as ridiculous or too risky. Pillay's offer had forced him into a position of no return.

He said "that's a very brave offer Pillay but if anyone is going to do it, it must be me." He stilled Pillay's objections. "The next question is, where is the best place to do it in order to minimise the risk to others. Though I believe the letters to be safe (God, I wish I did believe that he thought to himself as he said it) we have to allow for the outside chance that they are not."

They discussed various areas and finally decided on the hotel's freezer room. The hotel had a separate freezer room for food and drink. It was as solid a structure as they would find around the hotel. The room was detached from the other buildings and well away from the bedrooms so the guests could be kept away easily. They asked the hotel manager to come in. They explained the situation and asked him if they could have access to the freezer room. He reluctantly agreed to Hoareau using the room, though Hoareau would have used it even if he had not agreed.

Hoareau took the letters and a metal letter opener and headed for the freezer room leaving it t the others to clear the area and keep it clear. The story of the letters had already spread in that quick-silver way that exciting or dangerous stories can. Quite a large crowd had began to gather. I have to admit that I was there, even though I thought we were being rather morbid waiting to see if Hoareau blew himself up. We were kept well back from the freezer room so most of us went to the bar to wait for the next stage of the drama in comfort.

The freezer room was well lit thought Hoareau as he entered. At least, I'll be able to see what I'm doing. I should also keep my cool, its bloody cold in here. What a mess it will make if one of these letters is a bomb, he thought. He saw beer, wine, milk, sugar, jam, margarine, fruit, vegetables and cereals in a quick glance around the room. He found himself visualising the sight of bits of body - his body - mixed up with that lot, flying through the air. He mentally shook himself to remove the picture from his mind but the image persisted.

'I might as well get on with it," he said out loud to the empty room. "There is only one way to find out if it's safe to open them."

He laid the three letters on a shelf and looked at each of them in turn, trying to determine which one to open first. He decided, for no particular reason, to open them in alphabetical order. He picked up the letter addressed to the Botswanan Minister and turned it around carefully in his hands. It looked harmless enough.

"Here goes," he said out loud to himself and he picked up the letter-opener. I wish I'd got a plastic one rather than a metal one he thought, though he was not sure if it would have made any earthly difference. He placed the letter-opener slowly and gingerly in the right-hand top corner of the envelope and paused. Nothing happened. He found that his hands were shaking and tried to calm them. They would not stop shaking. If anything, the shaking got worse. I've got to go on now he thought. He very slowly pulled the opener down the length of the envelope. and then paused again. Nothing happened. He carefully prised open the envelope with the letter opener. Nothing happened. He eased his fingers into the envelope and carefully pulled out the contents, a single sheet of paper. Nothing happened.

Hoareau's heart was racing and pounding and he felt dizzy. He leant against the wall taking deep breaths for a few moments. One down and two to go he thought. He picked up the letter addressed to the Lesotho Minister and peered at it. It too -looked innocuous. He slowly repeated the four steps: opener entered at one corner (because Lesotho started with an L he superstitiously started the opening from the left hand side this time), the top of the envelope slit, the envelope prised open, the paper removed. Nothing happened.

He felt less shaky at the end of the second one and moved straight away to pick up the third envelope. Then he thought that it would be just like the South Africans to lull him by two safe ones and then hit him·with the third. He could not get this idea out of his head, even though he knew that he had determined the order in which he would open the letters, not the South Africans. He went even more slowly on this last letter than he had on either of the first two. Nothing happened.

He leant against the shelf when he had completed the third envelope successfully. He was bathed in sweat, despite being in a freezer. The operation had taken more out of him than he had expected. He found it difficult to summon up the energy to move. He wanted to look as composed as possible when he went out. He wanted them to think he had tackled the task calmly instead of becoming a jangle of nerves.

After a couple of minutes he found himself shivering with the cold. I can't stay here he thought. He put the letters back into their respective envelopes, picked up the three envelopes and the letter-opener and went and pressed the button by the freezer door, the signal that he was ready to come out. The hotel, sensibly, had such a device inside the freezer in case anyone was mistakenly locked in. It had proved useful on more than one occasion.

"They are all clear," he called as he was let out the door.

A large crowd of delegates and hotel staff had gathered quickly as they realised that the risk was past and they crowded forward and surged around him. Hoareau was slapped on the back, had his hand shook, was congratulated. He enjoyed the walk back towards the security room but all he said in response to the jumble of questions was "there was nothing to it." He formally handed the letters over to the representatives of the Botswana, Lesotho and Swaziland delegations outside the security room and then turned to the crowd.

"If you will excuse me gentlemen - and ladies," he added when he saw there were three women in the crowd, "I had better get back to work." Spontaneous applause broke out as he entered the security room with great dignity and closed the door.

The crowd slowly dispersed, still talking about the courage of Inspector Hoareau. They didn't know that as soon as he had got behind the closed door, he had collapsed in his chair and began to shake uncontrollably. His nerves had finally got the better of his willpower.

The delegates waited around in groups for some indication of the contents of the letters. Some details began to filter out that evening. It was not too hard to guess what the letters would say. All three of the countries were land-locked. Lesotho was right in the heart of South Africa, completely surrounded by several hundred miles of its large neighbour. Swaziland was only slightly less vulnerable. It was in the north-east of South Africa and just over three-quarters of its borders were with South Africa. The other border was with the southern tip of Mozambique. Botswana was much the larger of the three but it was sparsely populated as a large proportion of its land area was taken up by the Kalahari Desert. Almost half of Botswana's borders were with South Africa itself and another large part of them was with the area South Africa continued to control in defiance of the United Nations, Namibia. Botswana's remaining border was with Zimbabwe. Unfortunately for Botswana's security, their capital, Gaberone, was very near the border with Transvaal and therefore easily accessible to South African forces, as had already been shown by a raid into the Botswanan capital. The South African transport authorities provided all of the main transport routes for the three countries. They could, if they were of a mind, put the three countries under a virtual blockade. The South African power authority supplied all the electricity used in Lesotho, around 80 per cent of that used in Swaziland and just over half of Botswana's power. They could therefore black them out if they were of a mind.

The South African government had warned the US Congress when it was considering sanctions earlier in the year that an American decision in favour of economic sanctions could start a train of events that America would find impossible to control and had said that the worst effects would be felt by the independent black states of southern Africa. They had threatened to deport thousands of foreign workers if international pressure began to hurt their economy. There were about 350,000 foreigners working legally in South Africa but the number of illegal workers, mainly from the front-line states, was estimated at around two million. There was no way their home economies could reabsorb them if there was mass deportation So all three countries could scarcely be more vulnerable to South African pressure. The precise contents of the letters were spelt out to the Conference the following morning by the Secretary-General. They said that if those three countries supported sanctions South Africa would treat it an act of aggression and it would be retaliated. The Secretary-General said that though the letters did not spell out the nature of that retaliation, past actions by South Africa led him to believe that it would include military as well as economic retaliation. Conference delegates should consider the significance of that possibility he said. The delegations for Botswana, Lesotho and Swaziland were discussing the situation with their home authorities and would make a statement of their positions when the Conference resumed after morning tea. The South African threat had not come as a surprise to them. They had known that as the push for sanctions gathered strength, they could easily end up as the proverbial meat-in-the-sandwich. They had hoped they could continue to give general support to the objectives of sanctions without having to do much themselves. They had now been put on the spot.

Up until now, South Africa's immediate neighbours had generally participated in or responded to calls for sanctions in a more subdued manner than most of the other African states because of the vulnerable position they were in. The President of the Organisation for African Unity had recently renewed his calls for mandatory sanctions against South Africa following a _speech by President Botha. Botha's speech had been much heralded in advance as it was widely expected that he would set out forthcoming major constitutional reforms. The speech had been much criticised following its delivery for it failed to deliver any prospects of significant reform of the country's apartheid system. This failure had strengthened the pro-sanctions lobby considerably.

Many African states had strongly supported the OAU President's call for sanctions but these three front-line states had kept quiet. This wasn't regarded as surprising as no-one doubted that South Africa would retaliate against them if provoked. She had the power to bring the other economies to their knees if she wished. Though she would gain little from it except malicious satisfaction, such satisfaction would probably be sufficent motivation for South Africa.

The Zimbabwe government had made it clear that it considered the imposition of trade and other sanctions against it and the other so-called front-line states by the Pretoria government as inevitable. It had called on its people and the rest of the region to prepare themselves for a period of siege. They had also called on the international community to provide the finance and other help that would be necessary to minimise the impact of South African economic retaliation against them. The other three countries had, however. kept a low profile on the issue. If Botswana, Lesotho or Swaziland had any doubts about the inevitability of a kick-back against them, those doubts were now removed. They were in an unenviable position. If they failed to support the Commonwealth call for sanctions, the pressure on Britain and Canada to support the call would be lessened considerably. If they did support the call, South Africa had the power to cripple them and would almost certainly use that power. They would need financial help from the rest of the Commonwealth to meet the heavy costs that would fall on them. But the nightmare scenario that now haunted many at the Conference went beyond the need for financial help. South Africa had stated that those front-line states would be treated as enemies if they imposed sanctions. The retaliation could therefore be military as well as economic. Would the Commonwealth back the attacked countries militarily as well as financially? Few, if any, of the Finance Ministers at this conference were in a position to give any sort of assurance to the front-line states on that. The threatened countries were sceptical that much military support would be forthcoming if they were invaded. The rest of the world had done nothing to confront South Africa over their continued occupation of Namibia. To stop drinking South African wine or eating their fruit was a relatively easy thing to do. To send troops to fight in Southern Africa was infinitely harder. South Africa was increasing the stakes, an old poker playing gambit, though few thought she was bluffing.

The other African delegates knew that the carefully crafted consensus that had been emerging in support of sanctions was in danger of crumbling. Meetings between them and the delegations from the three threatened states had continued long into the night and continued in the morning. The issue was also a very complex and potentially explosive one for the developed members of.the Commonwealth. If they did not support sanctions, they could now be accused of bowing to the threats of force. If they supported economic sanctions but would not support the front-line states if they were attacked because of their imposition of sanctions, they would be accused of weakness and duplicity. If they went all the way, however, they may be committing their countries to participate in a war in southern Africa. They all had doubts about whether the vociferous public support that existed in their countries for economic action against South Africa would extend to support for military involvement. Particularly in Australia and New

Zealand, the legacy of those countries involvment in the Vietnam war lingered on in a strong and widespread anti- war mentality. The stakes had been increased for all players and the game, to use an analogy, for this was far from a game, was much more difficult and complex as a result.

These various dramas kept most of the delegates, including myself, up until midnight. I awoke the following morning in Simone's room again. When we had gone upstairs together after leaving the bar, she had quietly asked me if I was coming in again that night and I had said yes. It seemed the natural thing to do. If our love-making lacked the previous night's drama, it was still fresh and exciting. I had some moments of nervousness wondering whether the treatment I had received from the South Africans that morning would have affected my ability to rise to the occasion or whether the act of love would be painful. I was relieved to discover that neither was the case. I had not previously told Simone the precise details of what the South Africans had done to me. It had somehow seemed too personal. But as we lay together in the after-glow of our love-making I told her what had happened. She laughed and I was initially angry.

"It was no bloody laughing matter," I said in an offended tone. She comforted me in an appropriate fashion and I eventually saw the humour in the situation and laughed with her. I reacted to her comforting and we made love again. Maybe electric shock therapy was good for one's sexual performance.

When I woke in the morning, at 6.30am on cue, I again dressed quietly so as not to wake Simon, left a note, which was more personal this time, and crept out of her room. The same policeman was in the same place in the corridor. He gave me what I felt was an exaggerated 'good morning Sir' and a huge grin. I noticed that he addressed me in English this morning whereas it had been French yesterday. Cheeky bastard, I thought but I smiled back.

Fortunately, there was no message to contact the Minister that morning. I was getting tired of and embarrassed by the explanations of my absences to him, and this time I did not have an excuse. Nobody had shot at me, threatened me with a knife or applied shock treatment to me for twelve hours. I was, however, feeling very tired. The excitements of the last three days and the short nights were catching up on me. I felt I must be getting old.

Chapter Thirteen

ONE DOWN, HOW MANY TO GO?

If I was feeling tired, Inspector Hoareau was getting near the point of exhaustion. The letter-opening episode had been more emotionally and physically draining than he cared to admit. The reception he had received when he had emerged from the freezer with the letters had been a great boost to his ego but that had turned out to be the high point of the night. The rest of the night had been very frustrating. He had felt sure that he would be in a position to tell the President at his 7.00am briefing that they had picked up all or most of the South African agents so that the President in turn could tell the on Conference that it could proceed without fear of physical intimidation to consider a resolution on economic sanctions. He was not looking forward to informing the President that they had not done so.

They had picked up only one of them and they had killed one other. That left another four or five still at large. The rest had obviously been scattered and, hopefully, put on the defensive by the intense activity of the Seychelles police and army but they had not been caught.

Where could they go on an island as small as this with so many people looking for them, thought Hoareau. The trouble was there were about 3,000 tourists on Mahe island at any one time. Provided the South Africans acted sensibly they could easily merge in with the other tourists. After all, thought Hoareau, about 200 to 300 of those legitimate tourists would be South Africans. While most tourists to Seychelles came from Europe - from France, West Germany, Britain, Italy and Switzerland in that order of importance - the South Africans were second only to the Japanese as a source of tourists from outside Europe. So a South Africanin Seychelles was not exactly an oddity. That complicated the security forces' task.

They could have done the mass questioning bit and interviewed every tourist on the island. They would have had to go beyond those who had entered on South African passports as there was no guarantee that the terrorists had come in on such passports. In fact, Hoareau would have been prepared to bet that some of them at least had not used South African passports. He would have won his bet as the two men they had located during the previous night had both been travelling on British passports. But they did not have enough experienced men, even if he asked for the help of Llewellyn's British team and he was reluctant to do that, to question such a large number of people in a short space of time.

Also, the enforced police questioning of such a large number of tourists would have done their international image no good at all. They had put a lot of marketing resources into establishing the image of Seychelles as a warm, safe, easy-going holiday destination. Such reputations are hard to gain but very easy to lose. Tourists were the life-blood of the Seychelles economy. Even the publicity associated with this Conference would have an unfavourable impact on tourist arrivals for a while. When it came to influencing tourists in their choice of a holiday destination, the old adage that all publicity is good publicity was not true. Most of the stories in the world press from this Conference would be dominated by murder, shootings, motor-accidents, terrorists etc. The link between such bad news and Seychelles would be established in the minds of some would-be tourists. They would soon forget the details of what they had read but the unfavourable impression that Seychelles sounded like a dangerous place would linger on for some time. While the unfortunate impact mass police questioning would have had on Seychelles tourist industry may have influenced Hoareau's decision not to adopt that course of action, it had not been the main reason. Llewellyn had pushed· strongly for that course of action but Hoareau had argued that such an approach would take too long and was unlikely to work. The South Africans would have come in as legitimate visitors. With so many people to question, the questioning could only be cursory. As long as the terrorists remained calm in response to the questioning, they would not be identified by such a process. Llewellyn had said that he would be able to tell them immediately by the manner in which they reacted, it would not matter what they said. Hoareau had pointed out that it would not be possible for Llewellyn to do all of the questioning and other people would not have his 'skill' at picking out guilty from the innocent. Llewellyn had been too thick-skinned to realise that Hoareau was being sarcastic. Llewellyn had not been pleased with the decision not to carry out mass questioning but in the end had reluctantly admitted that the decision was Hoareau's. He made it amply clear, over and over again, that he disagreed with it and he would say so in his report on the Conference security arrangements to his Government.

Hoareau had believed that it was only by their actions that the South Africans would be revealed. He had been sure that as that night was the last one before the crunch day at the Conference, there would have been a lot of action from the South Africans during the night. There had been nothing besides the letters. He could not believe that they had given up so they must still have something up their sleeve. That worried him a great deal.

The two men they had caught during the night had given themselves away. The systems of surveillance they had set up in the hotels had worked successfully and led to the situation in which the two South Africans had panicked. The two had endeavoured to check into the Mahe Beach Hotel in the south west of the island at about 8.00pm without prior reservations. The police had a person on the registration desk of every hotel in Mahe. They were there to listen to accents, check passports and generally just watch and observe. As luck would have it, the two would-be guests approached the under-cover officer on duty when they came to the registration desk at the Mahe Beach Hotel. He asked to see their passports, which they gave him. He noted on the entry permit in their passports. that they had both. arrived in Seychelles four days earlier on the British Airways flight from Johanessburg. He also thought he detected a South African accent even though they had British passports which gave a London home address. He asked them, in a conversational tone, where they had been staying previously. All they had to do was give the name of some other hotel or guest house and say that they were shifting because it was noisy or dirty or had terrible food or some other such reason. The officer would probably not have checked such a story if it was presented plausibly. Instead, the two got flustered.

"That has got nothing to do with you' one of them said. "Have you got a room or not?"

The officer did not answer their question. He looked at them closely and said, "We are asking all guests the same questions for security reasons. If you have been here for four days you will have heard that there are South African agents on Mahe and we have to be very careful. So could you please tell me where you have been staying."

By now the attitude of the two had shifted from bluster to mild panic. The back one tried to whisper something to the one at the desk but was told to shut up by his colleague. "We are obviously not welcome here, we'll go somewhere else," he said and they picked up their bags and began to walk towards the steps down to the hotel's car park. The officer at the desk signalled the hotel security room, in which two other officers were on stand-by, and they called the Port Glaud police station, told them they had two suspects at the hotel and requested reinforcements.

The two South Africans continued to try and act as if nothing was wrong. They moved down the steps and across the garden towards the car park. There was a stream between the hotel and the car park which had only two bridges across it, a roadbridge and a footbridge. Both required a detour. The South Africans, obviously not knowing the gardens of the hotel well and not realising in the early evening gloom that the stream was quite wide tried to take the most direct route to the car park. They came up against the stream, stopped and swore.

It was not very deep and they could easily have jumped down into the stream and waded across. But that would have looked most unusual and at that stage they were still putting more emphasis on normality than speed. After looking around them and not noticing anyone observing them and not seeing anything else to alarm them they decided to follow the stream back to the footbridge. The delay was significant as it gave time for two cars of police from Port Glaud to take up positions at the main road entrance to the hotel.

When the South Africans finally reached the car park, security officers were already there. There were about fifty vehicles in the car park and the officers had not known which one the South Africans had arrived in. So they had decided to adopt a wait and see approach and had kept out of sight. The South Africans got into a roofless mini-make and quickly started up and drove out of the car park. The hotel drive had a sharp curve in it and a number of speed bumps that forced drivers to slow down if they wanted to avoid broken axles or bruised passengers. The South African's initial alarm had calmed down by this time as they could see no sign of pursuit and so they drove sedately. Their view of the main road was obscured by the curve in the drive and low hedges on either side of the drive. As they rounded the corner of the drive, however, they saw for the first time the police cars parked across the gateway, blocking off the end of the drive. They stopped. They looked behind them but they could not go back that way. For one thing, the drive was no exit and only led back to the hotel. For a second, another vehicle was coming slowly towards them. They could not see its occupants and it showed no obvious signs of being a police car. But the slow speed it was travelling at and the fact that it had no lights on led them to believe that was what it was. They were right. For a moment the two groups simply looked at each other.

Then the car behind the mini-moke turned on its lights, illuminating the South Africans clearly, and a voice called out "throw out your guns, climb out of the car and walk slowly back to this car." Both South Africans ducked down to the· floor of their vehicle. A mini-moke may have been useful as part of their tourist camouflage but it had decided drawbacks in their present situation. They discussed what they should do next. The passenger was for abandoning the vehicle and making a run for it on foot. He argued that the Seychellois police, "being darkies", would be too scared to follow them in the dark, particularly if they fired a few shots at them before they ran in order to increase their nervousness. The driver was not sure if the Seychellois would behave in the sameas their blacks and was not prepared to risk it. He did not want to abandon the vehicle. He thought it was their only chance to get away. They did not know the island well enough to travel on foot. He said the hedge alongside the drive did not look very dense. If they drove the vehicle through the hedge they should be able to by-pass the police cars at the gate and get on to the main road from somewhere else in the hotel grounds. There was a small drainage ditch between the drive and the hedge but the driver thought the vehicle would easily jump that. They decided to try it. They had left the motor running. The driver edged himself back up into his seat. His colleague, who had taken out a revolver, stayed down. As the driver reappeared, the same voice called out, "This is your last warning. Climb out of the car now or we will shoot. The second South African raised himself and shot first. He fired two shots in the direction of the voice and one at the lights of the ca r behind. He turned to face the front as the driver started the vehicle and picked up speed as he headed down the drive towards the police road-block. He fired two more shots at those police cars to keep them on the defensive.

When the mini-moke was about fifteen metres from the road-block, the driver spun the wheel sharply to the left and the moke bounced over the drainage ditch and hit the hedge, which offered little resistance. They broke through onto the hotel lawns. They nearly collided with one of the many coconut trees dotted around the lawns before the driver regained control. He slowed down and switched on his lights. "What's happening behind us?" he asked his passenger as he searched the roadside hedge, which was more substantial, for a likely spot to break through onto the main road.

"The vehicle behind us has stopped at the gap in the hedge. I think they're coming through on foot."

"Give them some hurry up," said the driver and the passenger fired a couple of more shots in the general direction of the other vehicle.

"The cars on the road are both facing the other direction. I think they may have hit each other as they tried to turn around," he laughed. He was right but it was not a serious knock. Both cars were still mobile but it had delayed their turn around.

"Now's the .time to go then" said the driver. 'I'm going through this hedge. Get down again'.

That was the last thing he said. He drove the moke at the hedge on a diagonal run. He had not noticed that unlike the first hedge they had gone through. which·was only decorative, this hedge had the job of protecting the hotel grounds from human and animal intruders and was helped in that job by a post and wire fence within it. All the wires except the top one were hit by the front of the mini-moke and stretched and broke. The top wire cleared the bonnet of the mini-moke, cleared the small front windscreen also but it did not clear the driver. It hit him right across the throat. His head was jerked back, his hands involuntarily let go of the steering wheel and his whole body was lifted out of the seat and flew out the back of the vehicle. He was dead before he hit the ground.

As the passenger felt the moke break through the hedge he gave a yell of glee and looked up. He could not believe his eyes. There was no driver in the vehicle and it was heading straight across the road for a stream, a continuation of the one that ran through the hotel grounds. The moke was slowing rapidly but the passenger was too disorientated to move quickly. Before he could raise himself and grab the steering wheel, the moke lurched off the road and fell nose first into the stream. He pitched out the front, losing his gun in the process and landed in the muddy water. He floundered around in the water for a moment or two until he realised he could easily stand up in the stream as it was only about three feet deep. He clambered up the bank and collapsed at the top. The police were waiting for him. He had no fight left in him. He was still at a total loss about the mystery of his missing colleague who had been literally with him one second and gone the next. He was dragged roughly to his feet and pushed into the back of one of the police cars. A policeman got in on either side of him. The car drove off to take him to Victoria· Police Station where Hoareau and his team would be waiting.

Behind them, with the drama over, one crowd of people began t? move down from the hotel and another to move along the road from Port Glaud village to examine the scene and try to find out what it had all been about. The body of the dead South African was unceremoniously bundled into the back of another vehicle to be taken to Victoria Police Station. They had no' need to wait for a medical expert to declare him dead. When the police had found him his head was almost decapitated. For some time it was a mystery to them how he had got in that state but they eventually located the three broken and one intact wires in the gap in the hedge where the moke had gone through and surmised what had happened. They had quickly covered the body and placed it in a vehicle before any of the public arrived on the scene.

The survivor of the two was now also having a rough time of it. One of the police officers escorting him was methodically hitting him, first in the ribs, then in the face, back in the ribs, up to the face, and so on. Each time he hit him he spat out, "you bastard." One of the shots fired at random by the passenger in the moke had found a human target, The South African made no effort to protect himself. He was still in a state of shock. No-one had yet told him what had happened to his colleague. For quite some time the other policeman ignored what was happening, though he did not join in. Finally he said, "let him be now."

"Why should I? He's a bloody South African spy. A few minutes ago he would have shot you and me if he could. He shot our friend Charles. Why should you feel sorry for him?"

"I don't feel sorry for him," he said, "But he's going to get a lot worse than you can evergive him before they finish with him at Victoria."

The captured South African was brought into Hoareau's office at the Victoria Police Station at about 11.00pm. He was looking considerably the worse for wear. Some of his bruises were gained from the car crash but Hoareau suspected that some of them had been inflicted subsequently by the angry police. He did not blame them or care.

The prisoner told Hoareau that his name was Piet Mulder. That was all he told them voluntarily. He refused to answer any other questions. If Mulder had looked bad when he arrived at the police station, he came to look worse and worse for wear as the night wore on. Hoareau's questioning was none too gentle. The pressure he and his men applied was straightforward – punches to the head and stomach, truncheon blows to the kneecaps and elbows. It got Hoareau nowhere. He did not really enjoy such tactics and at midnight he was pleased for once to hand over to Llewellyn, who had eventually been woken up. Llewellyn said that Hoareau was being much too gentle. There was only one thing that could make bastards like that talk and that was pain. There was no-one he could not break, Llewellyn boasted. He told Hoareau to go and have two or three hours sleep, a suggestion Hoareau gratefull accepted. During the next two hours Llewellyn and two of his men who were assisting him worked methodically on Mulder. They broke every finger on Mulder's left hand, they pulled his hair out in clumps, they pulled off three toenails. At first Llewellyn was cold and methodical but as Mulder continued to tell them nothing he became angry and brutal. His men tried to restrain him and were abused. It all. got him nowhere.

Hoareau tried again at 5.30am. Mulder was their only lead to the rest of the group. As no further developments had occurred during the night, they were more and more desperate to prise information out of Mulder.

Hoareau tried one last approach. He had the dead body of Mulder's colleague brought in. When Mulder saw the almost decapitated body he gagged and fainted. Hoareau had him brought round. The body still lay where Mulder could see it. He tried to keep his eyes off it but they kept coming back to it - he was mesmerised by the sight. Hoareau told him that that was what they had done to his colleague when he refused to talk. Was that what Mulder wanted also? This finally loosened Mulder's tongue but what he had to tell them was disappointing.

All Hoareau knew by the time he was finished was that there had been seven South Africans in all, including the Graylings who had been here for three months; the Graylings were the leaders of the team; that they had split up to make it more difficult for the police to trace them; that one of seven, Mulder's colleague, was dead.

They showed Mulder a number of photographs of people they thought could be part of the team, including some conference delegates and journalists who were not as far above suspicion as the rest. They were really on the list as long shots. Mulder was not a very good actor, at least by the end of the night. His eyes reacted to three photographs though his voice repeated, as it had for all the other photographs, that he did not know them.

Two of the three he reacted to were photos of Pieter and Sonia Grayling. They were already known to be part of the team. In the end, Mulder confirmed this. The third was a photo of a man called Daniel Braun, who had come in as a tourist on the same plane as Mulder. Mulder refused to admit he was part of the team but Hoareau was confident that he was. He had his photo copied and distributed to all units. They showed him photos of Snell and Miss Barnard but he showed no reaction to them.

Both Hoareau and Llewellyn had pressed Mulder to reveal what the South Africans' next move would be. Mulder simply repeated over and over that he had not been told about any further moves. He had been told to go to the Mahe Beach Hotel and stay there until contacted. He did not even know where the others were staying. Eventually Llewellyn conceded that that was probably the truth. Hoareau had reached that conclusion hours earlier. But neither of them believed that meant that the South Africans had nothing else in the pipeline.

Hoareau was trying to sort out these thoughts as he prepared for his Tuesday morning briefing of the President. If the South African 'troops' did not know what the next operation was, it could be something that did not involve them. What could it be? Blackmail - who, how? Maybe it was a target quite separate from the Conference site. Christ, he suddenly thought, that is why we can't locate them. While we are busy scouring Mahe for them, they may have shifted to Praslin or La Digue and will suddenly focus on some target over there. He doubted if they would have gone to any of the coral islands as they were too small and would be hard to get off quickly. But there were twenty or so flights a day back and forth between Mahe and Praslin and the police had only been watching the international flights. He realised that there were so many potential targets that it was pointless trying to guess what they might do. It remained a case of watch and wait, frustrating as that process was. There was no alternative.

He reviewed what he could report to the President. He could say that they knew there had been a team of seven, one was dead, one was in custody, they had identified three more. That left just two unknown members of the group. Both were males in their twenties. He did not know what they planned to do next. He was fairly confident however that they had not infiltrated the Conference, the accredited journalists or the hotel staff. Security at the Conference was as tight as a drum, though everybody would be getting tired.

"Christ, I know I am," Hoareau said to himself.

He looked at the clock on the wall. It said 6.45am. Only another ten hours to go and the conference would be over. He would be very relieved when that time came. I'm going to take a month off when this is finished and escape to La Digue, his home island, and do nothing but eat, sleep and walk. He often told himself that that was what he was going to do but he seldom got around to doing it. This time he meant it. He could already feel the peace and tranquility of La Digue beginning to envelop him as he thought about it. He had to shake himself and jerk his mind back to the present.

He was feeling far from satisfied with the progress that had made during the night and nervous as he left for his 7.00 am briefing of the President at the State House. Llewellyn had been keen to come also but Hoareau had not wanted Llewellyn to see his discomfort as he reported to the President and he was also afraid that Llewellyn would antagonise the President with his arrogance and confidence. The President could not stand smart-arses, particularly if they.were foreigners. The last thing Hoareau wanted right now was the President upset and making impossible requests of him .and his men. The main reason for Hoareau's nervousness was that he had built up the President's hopes and expectations when he had briefed him the previous day. The President in turn had spoken with great confidence to the Conference saying that they would have the South African agents in custody by the time the final day of the Conference commenced. Hoareau had only been able to deliver a very small part of what he had promised. The President would not be pleased and when he was angry he was unpredictable. He also had a long memory when it came to failure or disloyalty. He was not in the habit of forgiving either.

Chapter Fourteen

THE CANADIAN COMPROMISE

The second morning of the Conference opened at 10.00am with a statement on developments in the South African saga from the Chairman, President Baptiste. He had been scathingly critical of Hoareau's efforts during the briefing and following up a subtly injected hint from Hoareau, had switched his focus and remarked that the much-vaunted British assistance did not seem to have been of much help, a point of view Hoareau had quickly agreed with. However, in advising the Conference, the President put a very positive sheen on what had happened. He told them that they believed the South African team had consisted of seven people, two were now· dead, with a second one being killed in a motor accident at the Mahe Beach Hotel last night; two were in custody. The numbers he used included Snell and Barnard, even though he was aware that they were not part of the team'. He said the two in custody had given them the information necessary to identify the other three and he was confident that they had been effectively neutralised, though he would only be completely at ease when they too were in custody.

He said they had managed to take out of action four of the South Africans with minimal injury to civilians or tourists, the sole exceptions being the tourists, the British journalist they had shot and unfortunately, Thomas Bangura. The Seychelles police have not been so fortunate, he said. To date, three have been killed and two severely wounded in the course of their duties. He said he took great pride in the way the Seychellois forces had carried out their duties.

The Conference then moved on to other agenda items. They dealt with reports by groups of experts commissioned by the Commonwealth Secretariat on the world monetary system, the future role of the International Monetary Fund and the World Bank, and North/South relationships. Usually the debates on these issues would be long and intense but the few delegates who spoke only went through the motions. The ritual statements were made with only one from each side of the argument speaking as compared with the long line of spokesmen wanting to get their comments into the record at previous conferences. The reports were then noted, postponed to a future conference or referred to member governments for 'serious consideration' of what they could do to promote progress .in resolving the issue, generally a euphamism.for the issues being pigeon-holed.

These agenda items were like the curtain-raiser to a major sporting event or the warm up act to the performance of a big star. The audience could not wait for the preliminary to finish so the main event could get underway. There was time for only two speakers on the sanctions issue before morning tea - Canada and Fiji. There was considerable expectancy and uncertainty as Frank Clark, the Canadian Minister of Finance, rose and went to the speaker's rostrum.

He was a big man, with a big voice. After the usual introductory comments, he went through the efforts Canada and others had made at dialogue with the South African governments. He said their hopes had been raised by some modest changes in the internal policies in South Africa and it had been their expectation that the process of relaxing apartheid would continue at an accelerated pace. President Botha's recent speech had revealed that expectation, which South Africa had deliberately fostered, to be hollow and misplaced. Since that time, the pro-sanctions lobby had gained in numbers and strength around the world. Some countries, such as Australia, the Scandanavian countries and the United States, had taken limited action independently. He said he regarded the recent decisions of the United States as very significant, even though the actions announceed by the U.S. would not of themselves have very much impact on South Africa. The significance was in the change of approach that lay behind the U.S. decision. For four years their President had adopted a policy of 'constructive dialogue', which was the antithesis of sanctions. Contacts with South Africa had been maintained and even strengthened on the basis that private lobbying pressure on the Pretoria government rather than isolation of that government would be most likely to bring about apartheid reforms. That was a view the Canadian Government had shared.

"Canada still believes that trade sanctions are seldom effective; they are always discriminatory no matter how carefully they are designed and applied; they affect innocent people in other countries as well as the guilty in South Africa; and in South Africa they are likely to hurt black workers most of all. None of these concerns have been overcome by anything anyone has so far said at this Conference," Clark said. 'The aim of sanctions should not be to salve one's conscience. The aim of sanctions should not be to gain political popularity at home or diplomatic prestige abroad. The aim must be to force change on South Africa. If you accept that as the aim, then two principles follow and all here need to note these principles very carefully."

Clark paused and looked around the hall. There was now complete silence.

"The first principle is that in order to force change sanctions need to be toughly applied. I believe we should have no misunderstandings on this. The modest sanctions announced by Australia and the United States have been significant in.consolidating world opinion in favour of sanctions but they are little more than posturing as far as applying economic pressure to South Africa is concerned. They will have little or no impact on South Africa's economy. All those countries that are calling for the Commonwealth to apply mandatory sanctions, and that is most of you here, must mean what you say completely."

He looked pointedly at Baptiste as he said it. Baptiste was strongly advocating sanctions, but Clark was well aware that at present Seychelles imported a lot of their food from South Africa. Without saying it explicitly, Clark was telling Baptiste that these food imports would have to cease completely.

"Some have argued that the Commonwealth as an entity is finished if it fails to support action against South Africa. They may be right, though personally, I believe the Commonwealth would survive that disappointment. I have another scenario for you that I believe carries much more risk for the break-up. That scenario is that the call for sanctions is supported by this Conference, that the sanctions are applied

unevenly by the various countries in the Commonwealth; that some
countries even circumvent the sanctions and take economic advantage
of the situation. This need not be done in any official sense but by
commercial companies in some Commonwealth countries. If those
things happen, I believe it will lead to so much discord and anger within
the Commonwealth that the Commonwealth as we know it at present
would break up in bitter acrimony. A call for mandatory sanctions will
shift the Commonwealth into a position unlike any we have been in
before. It will put enormous pressure on Commonwealth solidarity and
I hope all of you who want to go that way understand the pressures that
will arise. I hope the Commonwealth is strong enough to withstand
them."

"So I repeat, my first principle for sanctions to be more than an
empty gesture they must be applied toughly and they must be applied
by all." Frank Clark paused and looked around the hall. He had their
complete attention now.

"The second principle is equally important. There must be a precise
objective that we expect the sanctions to achieve and the sanctions
must be withdrawn if those specific goals are met by South Africa."
He paused again to let that idea sink in. Then he said quietly, "I
believe that that principle has not always been applied with some of
the sports boycotts that have been applied against South Africa. Some
of them have had a shifting target. As the South Africans achieved
one target, another tougher target was set and the boycott remained
in place. None of those members who have so far proposed sanctions
have spelt out in other than very general term what they require the
South African governemnt to do to earn a remission of the sanctions.
Even New Zealand (I noticed Brian Franklyn stiffen) when it proposed
trade sanctions in twelve months time if South Africa had not moved
to start dismantling apartheid did not specify what moves would be
sufficient to avoid the imposition of those sanctions." Touche, I heard
Brian Franklyn mumble but he did not seem unduly upset.

Frank Clark paused again. Then he said, "I will now spell out the
Canadian position. The banning of new investment is an option that is
more clearly defined and more likely to be evenly and comprehensively

applied than trade sanctions. We would therefore support a call from this Conference for a comprehensive investment ban."

"On trade sanctions, we have some sympathy for the New Zealand position which holds such sanctions in abeyance for a year in the hope that they will be rendered unnecessary by the start of meaningful reform in South Africa. But we need to make it clear to South Africa what we mean by the start of meaningful reform."

"There is not sufficient time at this Conference to define that term and this is not the appropriate forum at which to do so. I would propose therefore that this Conference support the New Zealand proposal but with the rider that South Africa be told clearly and precisely what actions are required of her in order to avoid sanctions being activated in twelve months time. I suggest that a small group of experts be assembled by the Secretariat to draft a statement of the Commonwealth's requirements of South Africa and that this draft statement be considered by and finalised by a special Commonwealth Heads of Government meeting in December and conveyed to South Africa by the end of this calendar year. That would still give them over nine months to do what is necessary to avoid sanctions."

He wound up his address with a few generalities and returned to his seat. There was only a smattering of polite applause. Most delegates were trying to assess the Canadian proposal. It certainly was logical; it probably was fairer than any other proposal so far mentioned; but could it be made to work? Most delegates would have been hoping that this Conference would finalise the issue. The Canadians now proposed another, and possibly even more difficult round, to be fought out at a further Heads of Government meeting.

I sought out Simone at the morning tea break. The main reason was that I just wanted to be near her and talk to her. But I was also curious about how the Canadians had arrived at their position.

'None· of· your delegation said anything about this approach' last night," I said.

"We only finally sorted it out this morning. The Minister had not wanted to support sanctions at all initially," she replied. "Why did he change his mind?" I asked.

"Well, he spoke to the Prime Minister. I don't know what was said, but it was after that discussion that this idea began to crystallise. The Minister also read the mood of the Conference. Once the Australians and yourselves had supported Commonwealth action, we had no desire to be seen as the stumbling block to consensus." she said.

"You have left the British to face that.position alone," I said. "That's their problem," she said. "I think that Frank Clark secretly thinks that the Commonwealth will have so much difficulty in agreeing on an acceptable programme for reform in South Africa that the sanctions will never be applied. But I may be being unfair to him," she quickly added. She realised that she had been a bit too frank and that her Minister could well give her the sack if he heard that she was making such a suggestion about his motives.

"Frank Clark did say that the murder of the Gambian Minister had been major news in Canada and had made a strong impact on the public. The Prime Minister convinced him that Canada could not sit on the fence on this issue," Simone added.

"But you know that he wasn't murdered by the South Africans. Didn't you tell your Minister that?" I asked.

"No. How could I?" Simone responded. She was clearly upset by the question. "Did you tell your Minister?" she asked. I told her yes, though I did not tell her the circumstances in which I had done so.

"Why didn't you tell your Minister?' I asked. I realised as soon as I had asked the question that I should have let the matter rest. But it was too late now.

"I didn't know how to raise it with him. He had already heard the official version before I saw him. I did not know how to tell him that the official version was not true or how I would explain why I knew what had happened, so I kept quiet. They don't even know that the murderer was arrested in my room," she replied. She was angry with me for pressing her. Then she clearly had an after-thought.

"If your Minister knows, why hasn't he said anything publicly?"

Other people thankfully came up to join our table at that moment so I did not have to answer the question. I looked at Simone but she would not catch my eye. I could sense that she felt uncomfortable that

I knew that she had withheld what had actually happened to Bangura from her Minister. I in turn felt uncomfortable knowing that she now knew that my Minister did know what had happened but had chosen to say nothing. The easy relationship that had developed between us over the last three days now had to contend with an element of suspicion.

The one and half hour session between morning tea and lunch was a confused one. The Canadian proposal had thrown in the curly issue of determining exactly what was expected of South Africa. Most of the countries there would agree readily on the end objective, the dismantlement of the apartheid system. But there would be much less agreement on how fast that process should occur and how far South Africa would need to go before the economic pressure was eased.

Added to this conundrum, the South Africans threat to their neighbouring states had made most Ministers realise that by imposing sanctions they could end up getting embroiled in a military conflict in southern Africa, a prospect that appealed to none of them. The delegations from Botswana, Lesotho and Swaziland had not made a statement on their position after morning tea as the Chairman had previously said that they would. Instead, they had said that they were still in consultation with their home authorities and sought more time. They had said they would advise the Conference of their response to the South African letters after lunch. All of the other delegations felt sympathy for the predicament they were in so no-one objected to the delay. It seemed clear to most people, however, that the main reason for the delay was that they wanted to see which direction the Commonwealth was likely to go before committing themselves.

There was no point in their antagonising South Africa if the Commonwealth was not going to follow up with action that supported their position. The Ministers who were due to speak during this session all had their carefully prepared speeches which talked in generalities about sanctions and had not anticipated the very specific issues raised by the South African threats and the Canadian proposal. Most of them chose to read out their prepared speeches anyway, which gave this session of the Conference a curious air of being misplaced in time. As I listened to a lot of what was being said it was hard to escape the feeling that the previous session had been a dream. To be fair, most speakers generally added a sentence or two referring to the 'interesting proposal from Canada.' Most of them said they understood the points that Canada was concerned about but they would need to consider the proposal carefully as it was often difficult to be too precise when it came to political objectives. It would be a great shame if disagreement on specific points let South Africa off the hook when there was clearly overwhelming support for the general objective of forcing South Africa to abandon apartheid.

The one exception was David Crawford, the Minister of Finance for Jamaica. A group of delegates from African and Caribbean states had been meeting since morning tea to work out an attitude to the Canadian proposal. Crawford's speech was the last one before lunch and it clearly reflected the response of the hard-line states. These states also had to argue carefully and cautiously for if they rejected the Canadian or New Zealand proposals outright, both of which involved some deferment of action, they would end up with the Commonwealth divided on the issue.

David Crawford opened by saying he was grateful to Mr Clark for so eloquently reminding us that we are not looking for mere gestures. We fully agree with him that economic sanctions must be applied toughly in order to quickly achieve their objective. We are all conscious of the fact that the Rhodesian economy was more dependent on trade at the time Britain, in a move which we fully endorsed, applied economic sanctions against the breakaway white regime than is the South African economy now. Because those sanctions were not comprehensively imposed and were not enforced by some of the countries that did impose them, the Rhodesian economy survived a decade of sanctions by belt tightening and retrenchment. While the sanctions undoubtedly were important in the eventual transfer of political power in that country, and we were eventually able to welcome Zimbabwe back into the Commonwealth family, none of us can wish for a repeat of a decade of sanctions before change occurs in South Africa."

"As for Mr Clark's proposal for precise objectives to be determined by the Commonwealth and conveyed to South Africa, we can support the principle of what he is trying to achieve but we would caution against too great a degree of specification. There are many blueprints by which apartheid can be abolished in South Africa. We should not, from outside the country, endeavour to tell the South Africans the order in which they must do things. We all know where we want them to end up. I am prepared to allow them to determine how best to get there and I presume that Mr Clark would also be prepared to allow the South Africans to determine their own reform process by consultation among all the political groupings in that country."

He looked at Frank Clark and most other delegates followed his gaze. For a while, Frank Clark tried to remain passive and ignored Crawford's steady gaze. But after a time, he nodded his head in agreement.

Crawford continued, "It is crucial that the Heads of Government meeting be held this year. For the one thing in the proposals from both Canada and New Zealand that disturbs me is the delay both impose on the introduction of sanctions. I have two main reasons for my dislike of further delay. The first is that delay can become dangerous. If we cannot reach an agreed position this year, will we be able to do so next year? The facts of South African situation are, to use a pun, black and white. There is nothing more anyone should need to know. What is needed now is the political courage to back up the by now ritualistic verbal condemnation of apartheid with concrete action to change it. My second reason is the economic situation in South Africa right now. That country will never be more vulnerable to economic pressure than it is at this time. It is almost as if the business community of South Africa have been bent on creating the perfect conditions for economic sanctions to work. South Africa is being served notice that it cannot maintain its present system of apartheid and remain a fully paid-up member of the international financial community. Let me spell out for you what has happened," he said. "High short-term interest rates last year in South Africa led many South African banks and companies to foolishly rush to borrow short• term funds abroad where money was cheaper. The conventional wisdom in South Africa a year ago was that the rand would return to parity with the US dollar as the South economy expanded. Thus these borrowers would benefit from an exchange rate gain on repayment as well as low interest rates. Most of them did not take forward exchange cover, they were so confident of the outturn. So much for their conventional wisdom. But it is a graphic illustration of the arrogance and confidence of the South Africans that they saw the future of their country under apartheid in such glowing light that they were prepared to borrow so much in hard currencies and the South African authorities were prepared to sit back and let the debt build up. In all something like US $12 billion was borrowed short term and is due for repayment over the next eighteen months. As unrest has spread in South Africa, the brutality of the South African political system has become daily fare for the international TV news bulletins. As the number of coffins multiplied, the financial markets became nervous and the rand began to fall in value. Then the significance of the bulge in short term international debt repayments dawned on those markets and the run on the rand turned into a rout. Because those debts have to be repaid in US dollars or in deutschmarks or in Swiss that cheap overseas borrowing has become very, very expensive to repay."

"The South Africans are now in a state of panic. They are anxiously trying to buy time from the international banking community. They have two hopes. First, that the existing loans will be rolled over and the debt lengthened by rescheduling. Second, that the value of the rand will recover during the extended loan period and reduce the repayment burden." "Nothing speaks louder for the change in world opinion about South Africa than the way in which bankers, usually the most taciturn and conservative of people, are now publicly seeking to disown any responsibility for dealing with that country's debt problem."

"The Governor of the South African Central Bank has been travelling the world, cap in hand, trying to find a prominent international banker to act as a so called 'honest broker', a quaint banking euphemism for a pimp. At the moment, nobody seems to be very eager to take on the role, despite the obvious financial rewards. Someone will undoubtedly turn up but the fact that bankers are not falling over each other in their eagerness to get the position is significant. There is an old banking principle that says if you think there is going to be a panic, then it pays to be the first one to panic. Some major foreign banks have already withdrawn their deposits from South African banks. They have managed to achieve what politicians with all our talk have so far been unable to achieve - a form of economic sanctions against South Africa. They are self-imposed sanctions I know but they are still economic sanctions for all that. South Africa has frozen repayments of its short-term debts and reintroduced the two-tier rand system that it first used after the Sharpville massacre, twenty-five years ago. Banks also seem to be in the vanguard of disinvestment. The two major British banks in South Africa, have both recently had share capital raisings in South Africa. Neither parent took up its rights to the issues, thus voluntarily divesting themselves of their controlling stakes. While both banks deny that their action was a form of dlsinvestment, it certainly was not a sign of confidence in the South African economy and its present political system,"

Thomas Crawford continued. He dropped his voice and looked round the room. "Gentlemen, we should be ashamed that international bankers, probably the most conservative grouping of people in the world are doing more to put pressure on South Africa than are the governments of the Commonwealth."

He paused to let that sink in. Then he continued quietly, "one other important thing that these events have shown us is that South Africa is not immune to economic pressure. Those people who have argued that economic sanctions would have no impact on South Africa can no longer sustain their argument. South Africa will never be more vulnerable to economic pressure than it is now. The large amount of short-term debt it has puts it in a weak position to ignore sanctions. If the Commonwealth were to take the lead and strike a comprehensive blow now, there would be a good chance of achieving positive results quickly as South Africa is not in a position to fight a prolonged battle against trade sanctions. I am concerned that if we delay the imposition of trade sanctions for a year, as has been suggested by my colleagues from Canada and New Zealand, South Africa will have negotiated a rescheduling of her debts, tightened her exchange control and taken other actions that will allow her to stage a prolonged retrenchment against sanctions. This will only prolong the hardship the people of South Africa and her neighbours will suffer before they achieve equality and justice. If there must be a delay, let it be as short as possible. I do not understand those people who say that South Africa should be given a warning and time to start reforms. That country has received so many warnings over the past decades that it now routinely ignores such warnings as empty and null. It has had decades to start reform and has stubbornly refused to do so. I mentioned Sharpville earlier. Many of us thought that world opinion following Sharpville would force changes in the apartheid system. Sharpville was twenty-five years ago – twenty-five years," he shouted. "And some of you say that South Africa deserves to be given more time."

He stared pointedly at the British delegation before concluding. "I urge you to reconsider and support the imposition of comprehensive sanctions immediately the Head of Government have agreed on the aims of reform in South Africa."

He sat down to a standing ovation from most of the African and Caribbean delegations. The ovation was prolonged and many of the applauding delegates looked directly at those who were still seated. Brian Franklyn, noticing this attention, rose to his feet and the rest of our delegation had to join him. Most of the Asian delegations and the Australian and other South Pacific delegations also stood. The British and Canadian delegations remained seated.

The Chairman thanked Thomas Crawford for this statesmanship, his directness and his clarity. The alternatives were now clear, he said. He urged all delegations to consider carefully over the luncheon recess how far they could go towards the Crawford position as there was only the afternoon session left to resolve the issue. It would be a disaster for the anti-apartheid movement and for the Commonwealth if no agreed position could be reached. That would be regarded as a great victory by South Africa and would also strengthen the hand of terrorism everywhere as, whatever the Conference said, the world would believe we were intimidated by South Africa's crude actions and threats if we fail to impose some form of sanction.

It was a very thoughtful lot of delegates that filed·out of the Conference hall for lunch. The afternoon session was scheduled to begin two hours later and a great many formal and informal meetings had been set up or were in the course of being set up for the luncheon period.

Chapter Fifteen

THE IMPORTANT BUSINESS IS ALWAYS DONE AT LUNCH

One of those luncheon meetings was in the Chairman's suite. Present were the Ministers and aides from the countries that had been selected the day before as members of the committee that would draft the Conference communique. New Zealand had been put on that committee and Brian Franklyn was there along with John Kershaw and myself. Fortunately for me, Kershaw was the one who would have to actually work on the drafting committee. It was about time he did something, I thought. He had had a pretty easy time of it so far on this trip. He had tried to argue that I should be on the drafting committee because of my speech-writing experience but the Minister had told him to stop whinging and do some work for a change. Kershaw had not liked it. Then he noticed the look on my face. I had tried to hide my amusement but failed. That had made him boil but he was unable to say anything.

The other members of the committee were the host country, the UK, Kenya, Ghana, Malaysia, Solomon Islands, Bahamas and the Commonwealth Secretariat. As usual for such meetings, the first draft of the communique had been written by the Secretariat in London prior to the meeting. That draft set out all the sins of South Africa in the eyes of the Commonwealth and reiterated the Commonwealth's abhorrence of the apartheid system. There was little discussion or argument about those sections. It was only rhetoric. It had all been said before. The sections of the draft communique dealing with the Commonwealth response had not envisaged the changes in position that had so far occurred at the conference. It would need to be completely rewritten but it was still not clear where the consensus would lie or even whether a consensus would be reached.

President Baptiste spoke to Sir Robin Hollarn, the British Chancellor of the Exchequer. "We need to know your position in order to give the drafting group directions for their work," he said.

"It is not only our position that you need to know Mr President, there are some major differences between the New Zealand, Canadian and Jamaican positions and we do not know where a lot of other countries will come down," responded Sir Robin.

"I have already spoken to those three countries. There is in fact now little between them. The only issue is whether the South Africans have three months or six months in which to take action prior to sanctions being imposed following the transmission to them of the Commonwealth's position," said Baptiste. "Is that not correct Mr Franklyn?"

Brian Franklyn confirmed that it was correct. The Jamaicans, who he believed were acting as the spokesman for the hard-line states, would reluctantly accept a short delay and saw three months as the maximum. The Canadians and New Zealanders in turn had agreed to retreat from their position of twelve months to six months. They were to discuss the issue again at 2.45.

Sir Robin Hollarn looked around him arrogantly and began to speak. "I am surprised Mr Franklyn that you can so easily alter your position. We are all being pushed by emotion and sentiment into doing something that is in my opinion economically stupid and morally indefensible. Let us try and forget emotion for just a moment and use logic to examine the three actions being proposed."

He started with the proposed ban on new investment. "I personally am against such an action but it is the least objectionable of the three. At the moment most banks and would-be investors have imposed their own ban so anything this Conference does will be virtually redundant. My government has decided that it should not be completely opposed to all actions against South Africa. We wish to cooperate with the Commonwealth provided it does not compromise our principles. So we will not stand in the way of a ban on new investment for a defined period of time."

That was something at least. I had found the logic in this chain of reasoning hard to follow but I had often found that a politician's idea of logical thought processes was hard to follow.

He then shifted to disinvestment. "We do not and will never support disinvestment. There are a lot of reasons for this. Some of them you will say put my country's self-interest above all other interests. I make no apology for that. On this issue our self-interest is so much greater than any of yours. Britain has much more to lose than any other country from widespread disinvestment. For most of the rest of the Commonwealth it is an empty or inexpensive gesture. But not for us. British firms and individuals are the world's biggest investors in South Africa. That investment is tied up in factories and buildings that can't be moved. Do the rest of you seriously expect us to walk away from that investment.?"

Nobody answered him - he had not expected an answer.

"British people made that investment in good faith, long before South Africa came to be viewed as an international leper. My government is not going to tell them to divest themselves at whatever minimal price they can get. There is another argument against disinvestment that is even stronger than our own self-interest," he continued. "Mr Clark argued that if we are going to impose sanctions we must be tough. Mr Crawford agreed and also argued that if action is taken soon, there is a good chance of quickly forcing change on South Africa. It makes no sense to sell physical assets off cheaply to South Africans now and allow them to make a windfall gain in wealth when things start to return to normal in that country in six or twelve months' time. So I repeat, my government will not support disinvestment and I strongly suggest you leave it out of the communique."

"We will discuss that after we hear what else you have to say," Baptiste said. I suspected that he wanted some time to work out a suitable response.

"Very well," said Sir Robin. "For the third proposal, we are still very reluctant to support a mandatory recommendation on trade sanctions. You know the reasons for Britain's reluctance," he went on. "First, sanctions will hurt blacks more than whites, including the workers in British export firms, many of whom are black too." He seemed to think this last point had some special significance and having made it, he looked around as if expecting acknowledgement. He was disappointed. All he saw were grim faces.

"Second, a recent British study has shown that economic sanctions seldom work. I believe they worked in only about 30 per cent of the 100 cases in which they have been used over the last hundred years. Third, nothing has been said at this conference to change our view that sanctions are the wrong approach to adopt to the apartheid issue," he continued. "Frank Clark said some very interesting things and certainly helped to clarify the issues but the basic principle remains to be overcome and that is that we believe it is wrong to try and use economic sanctions to achieve political objectives."

"With all due respect Sir Robin," the Kenyan Minister interjected". "that statement cannot be allowed to go unchallenged. Your government used sanctions for political purposes against Rhodesia."

"That was not my government," Sir Robin responded smugly. "We cannot be held responsible for the actions of previous governments."

"Very well, but it was your government that used them against Argentina," the Kenyan Minister retorted.

"That situation was completely different," said Sir Robin, beginning to get nettled. "We were at war with Argentina." Before any of the African delegates could intervene with the obvious retort, he continued, "we are not yet at war with South Africa and we do not want to support policies that bring that possibility closer."

Recovering his poise, he went on. "Neither do we want to see war within South Africa. The recent tribal fighting in Nigeria, the continued fighting in Zimbabwe, Uganda, Mozambique, Angola, Chad., and in fact in most African states, show all too clearly the problems that could arise in South Africa if rapid reform is forced on that country. Other African countries are not immune to most of the criticisms levelled at South Africa."

I realised as I looked at him that he was actually enjoying himself now and was buoyed up by his own sense of moral superiority and the discomfort he was causing the others. There was a smugness about him that was very irritating.

"Just because some other members of the Commonwealth have altered their position", looking pointedly at Brian Franklyn as he spoke - Franklyn smiled back at the British Minister, forcing him to look away - "is no reason for Britain to do the same. I have no intention of being labelled as the British Minister whose actions led to a bloodbath in South Africa."

I was amazed. He was serious. One of his major concerns in this was how he would be viewed by historians.

"It may have escaped your notice Sir Robin, but there already is a bloodbath in South Africa. Over one thousand people have been killed in the last four months. That hardly seems like the outbreak of peace." President Baptiste remarked sarcastically.

"You are not in a position to preach to me Mr Chairman," Sir Robin retorted angrily. His face had gone very red and I thought he was on his way to a coronary on the spot. "I happen to know that the murder of the Honourable Thomas Bangura was not committed by a South African agent. You deliberately misled the Conference about that murder. How am I to know that the other so-called South African terrorist actions in Seychelles you have been telling us about are not also fabrications.?"

The other Ministers, except for Brian Franklyn, looked thunder-struck. Hollam's revelation was news to them. Baptiste had jumped to his feet, visibly very angry. "How dare you accuse me of deliberately misleading the Conference. At the time I made my statement on Thomas Bangura's murder I had not received the full security report from my officers. All I knew for sure was that Thomas Bangura had been stabbed to death. For the safety of all other delegates I felt it was imperative that that fact be conveyed to the Conference as soon as possible. It was an understandable assumption on my part that it was the work of the South Africans. I said what I did in good faith and with your safety in mind. It is still my belief that the murderer was acting on behalf of the South Africans." He stopped talking but remained standing.

"I accept that you acted in good faith Mr. President. But the Conference has still not been told that Bangura's murderer was one of his own delegation. Some ministers are still using the false information that he was murdered by a South African as a reason for justifying their support of sanctions. However, let us get back to the main issue. You wished to know my country's position on sanctions. At this stage, we consider that the Conference should go no further than the passing of a resolution condemning apartheid and asking each Commonwealth government to do as much as it regards as appropriate (or as little I heard Brian Franklyn mumble) in terms of economic sanctions to put pressure on the South African government to dismantle the apartheid system."

Sir Robin Hollarn sat back with a satisfied look on his face. He clearly felt that he had the upper hand. There was silence for a while as the others thought about their reactions. After moments during the morning when there had been great expectations of some significant decision, it now looked as if the Conference would end up with little or nothing except yet another general statement and with action left to be decided by the individual governments.

Finally, President Baptiste spoke again. He had by this time sat down again but he leaned forward and stared hard at Sir Robin Hollarn.

"Britain mistakes the depth of feeling of the rest of the Commonwealth," he said. He continued slowly and deliberately. "Most members are not going to accept a token statement of that sort. Britain's leadership of the Commonwealth is at stake. No, I believe it is more serious than that. Britain's membership of the Commonwealth is at stake. Indeed, the whole future of the Commonwealth is at stake. After all, what is the Commonwealth? Its membership has been determined by accidents of history. We remain together as a club because we can discuss issues and reach a consensus without the heavy political overtones of the other international forums. If we cannot reach meaningful positions on issues of crucial concern to ninety-five percent of its members, the Commonwealth becomes irrelevant and an anachronism. We will be no more than a mini- United Nations." Most of the other Ministers signified their agreement with this view. I wondered how Sir Robin Hollarn would like to be remembered by history as the person who destroyed the Commonwealth'

But Hollarn did not accept the Chairman's point of view.

"Such feelings of disappointment have existed before. They will blow over," he said blandly. "They always do. The ties that bind the

Commonwealth together are broader and stronger than any single issue."

"This time you will be mistaken Mr Minister," said the Chairman, but for once he seemed a little at a loss for words. In desperation he looked at Brian Franklyn with a look that seemed to say 'could you rescue the situation?' Brian Franklyn did his best not to notice the Chairman's unspoken plea so Baptiste put it into words. "Would you like to comment on the British position Mr Franklyn," he said. It was clear to me that at that particular moment there was nothing Brian Franklyn would like to do less. He looked most uncomfortable as he addressed himself to Hollarn.

"While I understand your concerns Sir, your concentration on the false accusation of the murder of Thomas Bangura seems to overlook the acts of sabotage and terrorism that can, without doubt, be blamed on the South Africans. One of your own countrymen is dead, my aide, Peter White has been attacked twice, three Seychelles policemen are dead and one is seriously injured. The direct threats to Botswana, Lesotho and Swaziland clearly come from South Africa. Canada and ourselves have also had threats. It is not appropriate for you to use the doubt about one incident to cast doubt on all these others."

The Chairman and the other African Ministers were smiling again and nodding their heads in support. Hollarn did not respond. Brian Franklyn paused. The others probably thought it was for effect - to build up the suspense before he delivered some telling point. But I had seen him in action at meetings too many times before to miss the signs. When he knew what he wanted to say he could not slow down. He prattled on without hesitation. A pause for effect and emphasis was something foreign to his speaking style. I knew that a long pause like this meant just one thing - he did not know that the hell to say next. He looked at me but I could not help him. This was between Ministers. Nobody else came to his rescue.

So he finally started again. "As for the significance of this issue for the Commonwealth, it would be the first time that Britain has isolated herself from all the other members of the Commonwealth. The other countries who share some of your concerns, like Canada, Australia, and ourselves have managed to find compromises that satisfy our sensitivities yet do not estrange us from the rest of the members. Britain is therefore the only one who is not prepared to search for such a compromise. The hardline states, who came here demanding immediate, comprehensive sanctions against South Africa, have had the sense to give ground and agree to a delay while the Commonwealth specified exactly what it expects of South Africa. Britain meanwhile stubbornly refuses to compromise. I urge you to reconsider. I believe the Canadian· position is the minimum that the Commonwealth can support. If you are seriously opposed to apartheid but wish to avoid economic sanctions, then you will have the opportunity to do whatever you can to get South Africa to start reforms prior to the deadline for sanctions."

He paused again. Hollarn still did not respond. Brian Franklyn's look in my direction was even more desperate this time. I had thought of a couple of things he could say but I had no way of conveying them to him unless someone else started·speaking and took the attention off him. His pause was interrupted by a knock on the door of the President's suite. Inspector Hoareau and Llewellyn came in. The Chairman gave them an angry "not now" and waved them out. They stood their ground.

"Sir, I apologise for interrupting your meeting but what we have to say is of the utmost urgency," said Hoareau.

"It had better be for your sake Hoareau," said Baptiste. I caught the look of intense relief on Brian Franklyn's face. He was being given time to think. He leant over and whispered to me "where do I go from here?" I said that Sir Robin had said that over the last 100 years, economic sanctions had only had a 30 percent success rate. That rate did not seem too bad to me. I suspected that it was a higher success rate than the multitude of wars and other military adventures for political purposes had achieved over that period. Brian Franklyn did not get a chance to make the point. Inspector Hoareau's next words changed the focus of the discussion abruptly.

"We have had a telephone call from a person identifying themselves as South African and which we have every reason to believe was authentic. He said there is a bomb planted in the Conference room and a second bomb planted in a site they won't reveal until they are satisfied that you have met their demands. They say they can detonate either or both at any time."

Everybody in the room gasped and some swore. Hoareau continued. "Their demands are that this Conference be terminated straight after lunch and that no resolution on economic sanctions against South Africa be put to the vote. They also seek the release from jail of Piet Mulder and safe travel out of Seychelles and back to South Africa for all of them.'

There was silence for a time which the Chairman finally broke. "Do you believe the bombs exist?" he asked Hoareau.

"I cannot rule the possibility out," Hoareau replied. "The Conference room has been thoroughly checked more than once by my men and by the British team. The room has been kept under very tight security at all times. I would say therefore that the chance of a bomb being in the Conference Hall is slight but I cannot say that it is zero. On the other hand, it would have been very easy for them to have placed a second bomb at some other site."

"What about you Mr Llewellyn," said Sir Robin Hollarn. "Do you believe the bombs exist?". Llewellyn looked carefully at Hoareau before he replied. It was obvious that there was something going on between them, something that was competitive rather than collaborative.

"Inspector Hoareau is too cautious I believe. My team and I have considerable experience in such matters. We have searched the room thoroughly every morning, including this morning. Our men are presently going over the room again. I am prepared to swear that there is no bomb in that room at present."

Other people began to respond. Llewellyn held up his hand. "Let me finish. I said I am prepared to swear that there is no bomb in the room at present. That, unfortunately, does not mean there might not be one in there when you meet this afternoon. The easiest way for a bomb to get into the room is for it to be carried in by one of the delegates. The delegates are only searched in a most cursory fashion and Ministers are not searched at all. We cannot be sure that all delegates are trustworthy."

Hoareau and others started to object but the Chairman held up his hand this time.

"Are you saying that they have a plant amongst the Conference delegates, possibly a Minister?" he asked.

"I am not saying that" Llewellyn responded pompously. "What I am saying is that that is the only way a bomb could get into that room. There need not necessarily be a plant. The carrier could be innocent and unaware of what he was carrying," replied Llewellyn. "The bomb could be quite small. The person could be carrying it in and out without realising. The only times we search the Conference room are when it is empty of delegates. There is no bomb there at those times, I can swear to that. But in view of the number of people who have access to the meetings and the limited or non-existent searches of those people as they enter, I can't be sure that there is no bomb in the room when the Conference is in session. If you believe all the delegates and other people who have authorised entry to the room are safe and above suspicion, then you can work on the basis that the bomb threat is a bluff. If you are not 100 percent sure of that, and I am certainly not 100 percent sure, then you will need to search everybody going in carefully and methodically in order to be sure that there is no bomb in there. If you permit me and my team to search all delegates, including Ministers, going into the; afternoon session then I would be prepared to assure you that there will be no bomb in that room."

Baptiste looked at Hoareau but the latter declined to comment. It was Baptiste who spoke again.

"Well, Mr Llewellyn. While your assurance displays a great deal of confidence on your part, it is still only a conditional assurance. It is valid only if certain actions occur. That means that neither of you can rule out the possibility that there may be. a bomb in the hall. I think we therefore have to proceed on the basis that the bomb threat may be real. Are we agreed?" There were murmurs of assent and no dissension.

Llewellyn started to speak again but Hollarn quietly told him to wait.

"Assuming there is a bomb in the hall, do you think the South Africans would use it if we ignored their threat and continued with the Conference programme,?" Baptiste asked of nobody in particular. Nobody was in a hurry to answer him.

"Sir Robin," Baptiste finally said, "Do you believe the South Africans would use their bomb if we proceed?"

The earlier smugness had gone from Hollarn. He looked the Chairman squarely in the eye and took his time in replying.

I could see that Llewellyn was trying desperately to catch Hollam's attention but Hollarn ignored him and continued to look thoughtfully at Baptiste. Finally he said, "yes, I think they would." There was a snort of disgust from Llewellyn but Hollarn continued to ignore him.

"And what is your view now of the South African government?" the Chairman asked Hollarn. "Do you think they are deserving of your sympathy? Do you believe you can talk persuasively to a government that would use such a tactic against a meeting of Commonwealth Ministers?"

Again Sir Robin did not reply immediately but he continued to look directly at Baptiste. By now both Llewellyn, Hollam's Principal Secretary and Andrew Mayhew were all trying to catch Hollam's attention. I overheard his Secretary whisper to him that they needed to discuss the implications of what had happened before Sir Robin answered but Hollarn ignored him. "No," he answered to Baptiste's questions. He went on, "They have gone too far this time. It is us·they have now painted into a corner. If we oppose a Conference resolution on sanctions they will believe it is because of the fear of their bomb threat to us here and the threats to their neighbouring countries. If this Conference fails to take some action and subsequently my country or any other country of grouping of countries tries to exert pressure on South Africa in any other way to change their policies, they will undoubtedly resort to threats and violence again. Not only would a weakness now by the Commonwealth encourage the South Africans to greater use of terrorist tactics, it would give an unwanted boost to terrorism everywhere. I therefore feel that I have no choice. I will support the Canadian position if we can find a way to put a resolution.'

"Thank.you very much," replied an obviously relieved Baptiste. While the expressions on the faces of most in the room were one of relief or satisfaction, the expressions on the faces of Llewellyn and Hollam's Principal Secretary and Andrew Mayhew were quite different.

Llewellyn's mirrored anger, the others amazement. I wondered if Hollam's last few words meant that he believed he would get off the hook because the Conference would need to be called off because of the bomb threat and no resolution would be able to be put. It seemed to me that whether or not a resolution was passed this day at this place was not that crucial any longer, provided nobody subsequently changed their mind. It would be much cleaner and clearer if a formal resolution was passed, but even without it, an agreed compromise position had been reached and the Commonwealth governments could endorse it in a number of ways. They did not· all have to be together or do it simultaneously.

Everybody in the room began talking at once. I was close enough to overhear a whispered conversation between Hollarn and his Principal Secretary. The Secretary whispered, "Sir, you have just committed the government to something they have explicitly and consistently opposed."

Hollarn replied tersely, "We have changed our minds before. Knowing when to change one's mind is the art of politics, something the Prime Minister has still to learn and probably will never learn. I had no choice but to change our position in the circumstances. If I had not the rest of the Commonwealth - and the rest of the world - would have seen us as and publicly described us as apologists for and defenders of terrorism. Besides, I have not actually committed us to anything. The whole issue goes from here to a Heads of Government meeting before any sanctions are finally agreed upon or imposed. If Margaret wants to stubbornly stand her ground, let her do it then."

"We must inform her immediately Sir. She will be very angry," said the Secretary.

"I do not fear her anger any longer. If she over-reacts it is more likely her who ends up being isolated by the issue," Hollarn replied. "You phone Downing Street as soon as we get out of here.' His Secretary tried to object and argue that the Minister should speak to the Prime Minister directly but Hollarn was no longer listening to him. He was talking animatedly to the Kenyan Minister who had come up to shake his hand and congratulate him on his decision.

When the Kenyan Minister left to talk to Brian Franklyn, Mayhew and Llewellyn, who had been conversing quietly together, came up to Hollarn. Both were angry, Llewellyn much more so than Mayhew. But it was Mayhew who spoke first. "Sir, I believe you have made a major mistake. The previous British position on sanctions has been carefully worked out over a long period and has been resolutely adhered to by the Government in the face of Commonwealth criticism. It is a mistake to alter that policy on the spur of the moment because of one or two incidents. With all due respect sir, I also believe you have overstepped your authority. I urge you to reconsider and advise Baptiste now that you have to consult with London before things advance beyond the point of no return."

Hollarn looked at Mayhew with scarcely disguised scorn and said "things have already passed the point of no return Mayhew. But you need not fret. It is not you who will be held responsible. I am perfectly happy to justify what I have done to the Cabinet and, if necessary to the British people.'

Andrew Mayhew started to argue further but Hollarn cut him off with a curt "I do not want to discuss it further Mayhew. It is done."

By now Llewellyn was shaking with anger and could scarcely contain the anger as he whispered.

"Sir, you have chickened out for no reason. There will be no bomb in that hall. I can make sure of that. There was no reason for Britain to give in and support a bunch of wogs against South Africa." Hollarn looked at him stonily and said,

"Don't you dare talk to me like that again Llewellyn or you'll find yourself out of the service on your ear," and he walked away. I heard Llewellyn mutter "I'll get you first you bastard.'

History is often determined by quirks of timing. Had the South Africans held their hand for another two hours, Sir Robin Hollarn would have reiterated Britain's opposition to the use of economic sanctions and any hope of a unanimous resolution of any substance would have passed. By their bull-headedness, they had made certain that the opposite outcome to the one they wanted eventuated. There must have been many such moments throughout history where had certain events or actions have been delayed by even an hour or two, the future path of events would have been quite different. It became clear to me as everyone talked that a second, small bit of history had also been determined by that accident of timing. The Ministers from Kenya and Ghana and President Baptiste had all come up to Brian Franklyn and shook his hand warmly and congratulated him on his contribution. He looked a little bemused but no politician is averse to accepting congratulations, even if he is not entirely sure what he is being congratulated for.

It became clear that Franklyn was regarded as a statesman and something of a hero by Baptiste and the other Ministers. He had taken their side against the British and by his logic helped to force Hollarn to reconsider his position and change his mind. Only Brian Franklyn and I knew that he had been playing for time, had had no idea how to continue his arguments against the British position, and had been about to give up the attempt when fate intervened in the person of Inspector Hoareau and his crucial message. The Chairman finally called the group back to order.

"Gentlemen, we need to decide what we do now," he said. "We have agreed that we must act as if the bomb exists. But if we proceed and tell the South Africans we are ignoring their threat, what would they gain by detonating the bomb here or the other one, wherever it may be. The agents here could not take such a major step as blowing up all the Commonwealth Ministers of Finance without clearance from Pretoria. And even that mad Government would surely not order such an act. It would isolate them entirely. The Americans, the Japanese and the EEC would all have to isolate and bring down such a government. The South Africans would have nothing to gain and everything to lose by detonating the bomb."

Most of the other Ministers nodded but none of them seemed keen to state an opinion. Finally Hollarn said, "we will need to inform all delegates of the threat and give anyone who wished to leave the Conference because of the threat the opportunity to do so."

The others readily agreed to that. Then Wesley Braithewaite, the Minister of Finance for the Bahamas, said, "I do not think we should confront the South Africans as directly as you have suggested Mr Chairman. I have an uneasy feeling that they may carry out their threat if we do confront them for they will feel that we have painted them into a corner in which they cannot show weakness. If we are to proceed with the Conference, we should be very careful and try and bluff the South Africans into thinking that we have met their demands." Most others thought his suggestion was worth adopting, even though they did not agree with his reason for suggesting it. Most still thought that the South Africans would not detonate the bomb as they would have nothing to gain from such an act.

I decided to speak. "The South Africans may not decide their response in terms of gains and losses to themselves in the way most other people would. If the Conference proceeds they will know that they have failed to deflect the Commonwealth from imposing some form of economic sanctions against them. That will be a great psychological blow to them and a strong signal to the rest of the world. They will have lost the battle of wills. They will therefore see all of you who took that decision against them as enemies of the South African state. Their actions against you may be based more on motives such as revenge and retribution. Such motives feature strongly in their history and in the current rhetoric of their leaders when they have been justifying their incursions into neighbouring states. I for one therefore believe they would detonate the bomb. I won't attend.this afternoon's session if you proceed. I am already well aware from personal experience that the South Africans have, a strange conception of morality."

I flushed and stopped talking. My intention had been to say that they did not need to confront the South African threat now that they had reached an understanding on Commonwealth action. That understanding could be formalised some other way. But I had got carried away and started talking about myself. I should have kept·my mouth shut in this company. I had not even realised myself when I started talking that I was going to say that I would not attend that afternoon's session. As I spoke about the South Africans, my personal fear of them had asserted itself and the words had just come out.

The Chairman looked at me sternly. Brian Franklyn looked at

me with surprise, probably as much at my nerve for speaking at all as at what I had said. It was Baptiste who responded. "I appreciate Mr White's personal feelings. He has had some very unpleasant experiences during the last few days. I do not blame him for wanting to opt out. As Chairman, I have no objection if you do not attend and I am sure Mr Franklyn will not object either." Brian Franklyn was taken by surprise but agreed. That saved me having to argue about it with him later. The only one who did argue about it later was John Kershaw who, predictably, took the opportunity to comment on my lack of nerve. President Baptiste then continued. "The rest of us cannot take Mr White's easy way out," he said rubbing the salt in. "What I propose for the rest of us is the following:

First, that ·the police immediately search the conference room - again"

"That is already being done," Llewellyn interjected. Baptiste looked at him with distaste and said "Do it again". Llewellyn opened his mouth as if to argue but then thought better of it.

"Second, all delegates going into this afternoon's sessions should be carefully searched by Inspector Hoareau's men. I will explain to the Conference why it is necessary. I will be surprised if anyone objects." Llewellyn again started to argue that he and his men should do it but Hollarn spoke over the top of him.

"That means that you see this afternoon's sessions as proceeding?" asked Hollarn.

"Yes I do" said the Chairman. 'I will explain the circumstances as I go. It will be clearer if I could set out the whole of my proposal and we discuss it at the end." Nobody disagreed, though Hollarn looked irritated at the slight. Baptiste decided to placate Llewellyn a little.

"We would be grateful if the British security team assisted in the search of the delegates.' Hollam agreed. Llewellyn said nothing.

"Third, I will inform the Conference of the bomb threat and, as Sir Robin suggested, offer delegates the choice of leaving there and then."

"Fourth, Inspector Hoarea will contact the South Africans - you can contact them Hoareau I assume?" he asked.

"No, I cannot contact them but they are to call me again at 2.45 to get our response," replied Hoareau.

"That will do," said, Baptiste. "You will tell them that their demands will be met. There were one or two exclamations of surprise but Baptiste held up his hand.

"Please wait until I have finished. I do not intend that we actually meet their demands, only that, as Mr Braithewaite suggested, we tell them that we will do so to gain some time. Now Hoareau, you tell them that we are prepared to release Mulder. He would be a damn embarrassment to us anyway. Ask them where they want him released and how. Try and get them to agree to a release this afternoon. That may divert their attention for a while. As they will still be on the island, we will be able to arrest them again later is we so wish - won't we Inspector?" Baptiste said. Only Hoareau knew the reason for the last comment and that it was a criticism rather than a question. Hoareau simply nodded.

"You will also tell them that the Conference will go into its concluding session straight after lunch and that I, as Chairman, will explain the new situation to the delegates and tell them that the South African sanction issue it to be shelved," the Chairman continued. "Tell them that we will instead conduct the closing business of the Conference and will wind the whole Conference up in one hour. You can try telling them that would guarantee there would be no time to finish the debate on sanctions and reach consensus on a resolution as a number of countries, including Britain, have still to speak and put their position and they are not going to give up that right."

"Fifth, Sir Robin Hollarn will be given the opportunity to make a brief statement to the conference of the British position. I think that will be necessary for us to reach a quick consensus but please be brief Sir Robin. We will not have much time. Will five minutes suffice?" he asked.

"Yes, in the circumstances that will do," Hollam replied.

"None of the other countries who have not yet spoken will be allowed to speak' Baptiste went on. I will try to contacttheir Ministers before the session starts and explain why. We will have less than an hour to complete our business. We will need to be out of the hall by the time the time-limit we have given the South Africans is up, just in case their threat is a real one."

No-one argued with that, not even Llewellyn, who seemed to have given up arguing but still looked very annoyed.

"Sixth, once Britain has spoken, I will put the Canadian position to the Conference for unanimous support. I am not aware of any country that will not give that support now that Britain has come round. Do any of you foresee any problems" he asked

"Not major problems but there could be a few uncertainties about the reaction of Botswana, Lesotho and Swaziland. They asked for more time to work out their position this morning. I expect that now we have Britain's support they will display solidarity despite the risks to themselves. I will check that as soon as we finish and let you know if there is any problem Mr Chairman," said the Kenyan Minister.

"We all tend to forget that there is one African member of the Commonwealth that takes a different stance on this issue to the rest. Malawi has not yet spoken here and they have kept very quiet so far. But their position in the past has always been against sanctions," Hollarn said.

'! Sir Robin, could you have a word., with their Minister prior to 3 pm? They are more likely to listen to you than anyone else," said Baptiste. Then he added "even if you cannot shift them from their position, I do not think a resolution that has everybody's' support except theirs will be materially weakened by their non-support.'

Hollarn agreed to try some gentle persuasion.

"The other three countries are meeting again now. It may be a good idea Mr Kiungu if your colleague, Mr Wamalwa, left this meeting now and went to their meeting and explained the new situation regarding the bomb threat. One option that they may wish to consider is taking advantage of my offer to leave the Conference because of the threat. They would thus avoid the need to explicitly vote in favour of the sanctions resolution. Tell them that if they choose to adopt that course, the rest of the Commonwealth will understand and support their decision. Do the rest of you agree with that?" Again, no-one argued.

"Seventh, once that resolution has been put and passed, I will immediately close the Conference and we can disperse. I can forego the usual votes of thanks. The others that we traditionally thank at the end of these conferences can also forego their thanks. The South Africans will be giving us one hour. We should be able to complete the necessary business in not much more than half-an-hour, provided nobody argues. Then that leaves time for those who want to get as far as they can from the Conference Hall and it's alleged bomb to do so."

It was a masterful performance. He had thought of everything. The other people at the meeting had no comments to make and they readily agreed to the programme as laid out by Baptiste. The only question of substance related to the second bomb the South Africans had mentioned. The Bahamian Minister, Mr Braithewaite, asked "in our concern for our own safety we seem to have forgotten that the South Africans claim that a second bomb has been planted somewhere else. What do we intend to do about that second bomb?"

Nobody answered immediately so Baptiste looked at his Inspector and said "well Hoareau, what do you intend to do about it?"

"Until we know something about its location there is really nothing we can do. When I speak again to the South Africans and tell them that we are meeting their demands I will try and get them to tell me where the second bomb is. But at the moment there is little we can do, other than to warn all our officers and to carry out some limited searching at possible targets," said Hoareau.

"That seems to mean that we here will bluff the South Africans and clear ourselves out of danger but when they find out they have been bluffed they will still have their second bomb with which to extract revenge. We are saving ourselves but deliberately putting others at risk," Mr Braithewaite persisted.

"What do you expect us to do, give in to the South African threat?" asked Baptiste.

"No, just warn other people besides ourselves and clear them from danger too," Braithewaite said.

"Warn who? Let's be realistic," replied Baptiste. "Hoareau will do his best to get more information but at present there is nothing we can do. If we issued a general warning that there is a bomb planted somewhere on the island but we don't know where, we will have a panic. We don't even know if it is on Mahe. It could easily be on another island. What can people do with vague information like that to save themselves. They are just as likely to go towards danger as away from it. Do you think I am not conscious of what an explosion amongst the local population or tourists will mean for the image of a peaceful, tropical holiday paradise that this country is trying to foster abroad. But what can I do at this stage to prevent it Just tell me that." Baptiste was getting angry. Brian Franklyn tried to calm the situation.

"Mr Bralthewaite," he said, "while we all agree that the South AFricans are now little more than terrorists, there is still a distinction between their actions and the actions of many other terrorist groups. I think I am correct in saying that the South Africans on all occasions have aimed their retribution, revenge or pre-emptive strikes against groups or people they perceive to be enemies. They have not yet resorted to indiscriminate attacks on civilians or innocent groups in the way that many other terrorist groups do, even though sometimes civilians have been hurt in their attacks. On that basis, while we in the Conference have every reason to fear their retaliation, I think it is unlikely they would use their second bomb, if it exists, as a form of retaliation. It would be out of character with the way they have so far operated and would destroy any facade of civilised behaviour their government had."

There was general agreement with his point of view, though Wesley Brathewaite remained unconvinced. It was not clear to me, however, whether the others agreed with Franklyn out of a conviction that his description of South African behaviour was a correct one or simply because his argument got the problem off. their plate. I suspected the latter.

Chapter Sixteen

THE FINAL SESSION

So that was what they did. They proceeded with the Conference session and tried to telescope the finalisation of a resolution in favour of Commonwealth sanctions against South Africa into a half-an-hour's discussion.

I went to the beach. Simone came with me. I had explained the situation to her after the lunchtime meeting and she had decided to opt out as well. I saw a few other delegates walking around or on the beach too, including most of the Bahama delegation but not their Minister. However, most of the delegates had decided to be brave and remain in the Conference Hall. Even the delegations from Botswana, Lesotho and Swaziland had decided to remain despite the obvious attractions as a possible solution to their dilemma a withdrawal from the final Conference session would have offered.

I was the only member of the New Zealand delegation not to attend. I was sure Kershaw would remind me, and others, of that over and over again when we got back to New Zealand. I admit I felt a bit of a heel and coward sitting on the glorious sand of Beau Vallon beach while the rest of them were in the Hall. The Minister had not tried to get me to change my mind, though Trevor Barnes said I was making both myself and New Zealand look stupid. But the Minster's look as they went off towards the Hall and I headed for the beach indicated clearly that he thought I hadover-reacted and was acting foolishly.

Once or twice I almost convinced myself that I was being naïve and should put on a brave front and go into the Conference. I had the silly idea that my non-attendance may have been noticed and could be affecting Conference morale and solidarity. I soon realised that was nonsense. Only a handful of delegates would notice I was not there and my absence would only be a curiosity to them. Besides, I was in my togs. I couldn't go into the Conference dressed like that or my presence would cause more of a stir than my absence. By the time I changed clothes, the Conference would be over so I stayed on the beach with Simone.

Simone and I did not talk much but for some reason there was less strain between us than there had been earlier in the day. The periods of silence were not embarrassing, they were companionable. Only with people with whom one has a close rapport can silence be a form of communication, a way of enhancing the feeling of closeness.

We were both waiting for the Conference session to finish so that the tension we felt could begin to ease. Neither of us felt like swimming despite the heat and the beautiful water. Simone jokingly asked me if I felt like going paragliding again but I did not appreciate the joke – and told her so. So she called me a grump and left me to my thoughts.

I thought about President Baptiste's performance at the lunch-time meeting. It had been so good, so well-organised and so firm that I began to wonder if the whole bomb idea had been an elaborate hoax by the Seychellois, and maybe others in collusion, to force the hand of the British. There had been so many twists and turns to the events of the last few days. My mind began to try and sort out how they could have worked such a hoax. It would have needed very good timing.and Baptiste and Hoareau would have needed to be very good actors. Both of them had shown on occasions that they were good actors. So maybe, just maybe they could have worked such a hoax successfully.

I turned to Simone to try the idea out on her. I began to say to her that I was thinking the bomb may have been a clever hoax – when I got the clearest possible sign that it wasn't a hoax. A loud explosion tore through the air. I had never heard a bomb before and the noise was hard to describe. It was like thunder, only magnified. Unlike thunder, there was no warning, no obvious build-up of sound and it was so close that it was much more menacing than thunder. The explosion was followed by the sound of falling masonry andtimber and screams – screams of panic, screams of fear, screams of pain. They all intermingled into a spine-chilling symphony.

While most other people were rushing away from the scene of the explosion, Simone and I pushed our way towards the Hall. Neither of us expected a second explosion here and we were anxious about our colleagues who had been at the meeting. The scene at the Hall was less dramatic than I had anticipated. By the time we got there, the initial collapse of the Hall had subsided and only the dust was still falling. The Hall was separate from the rest of the hotel and only linked by a covered walkway so there was no damage to other hotel buildings.

The screams of panic and fear had also subsided and the screams of pain had been reduced to moans. The local police would not allow us near the Hall but we were told that most of the delegates had left the Hall before the explosion. We headed to the lobby and we met some members of the Canadian and New Zealand delegations tentatively approaching the Hall from that direction.

Over the next hour or so, as emergency services swept into operation to clear the rubble of the collapsed Hall and deal with the wounded and dead it gradually became clear what had happened. The Conference had finished its work as set out by the Chairman at lunchtime. There were no delegations that chose to miss the session in total but many delegations were below full strength. Sir Robin Hollam had spoken and endorsed the Canadian proposal. The Chairman had asked the Conference if there was any delegation that did not support the Canadian position. The Secretary-General had read out exactly what that position was. Canada and the hard-line states had compromised on giving South Africa four months to react positively once the Heads of Government meeting specified precisely what the Commonwealth expected of South Africa and the Heads of Government meeting had to held within two months.

There had been no voices in opposition, not even Malawi. The Chairman did not put the proposal to a formal vote but declared that it had unanimous support. The Chairman had been able to conclude the session in just twenty-two minutes.

They had not actually cleared the Hall area. Hoareau had not attended the session. He had left to try and track down the South African terrorists from clues he had gleaned from his second phone call with them. He had left the arrangements for clearing the Hall to his assistant, Auguste, with the help of Llewellyn and his team. Llewellyn had decided that as the search of the Hall before the meeting by him and his team had turned up nothing and asthe only way for a bomb to get in subsequently was with one of the delegates and they had all been searched, no bomb existed and there was therefore no need to force evacuation of the area. Hoareau's assistant hadnot been sufficiently confident of his authority to act to overrule Llewellyn.

Fortunately, Baptiste had made the threat very clear and graphic in his speech and most delegates had left the Hall at the first opportunity. But a small number were not so sensible or fortunate. Some had stayed on in the Hall itself and others in the foyer to chat about what had happened. They included three of the group that had drafted the communique, including John Kershaw and Andrew Mayhew. They had still been in the Hall when thebomb exploded and were now beneath the rubble. Little hope was held for their survival.

It was unclear how many other delegates had remained in the Hall. All the Ministers had left. However, some officials had remained talking or sorting out their delegation's papers. Two members of the Indian delegation and one each from the Fijian, Mauritian, Sri Lankan, Malaysian and Singaporean delegations were unaccounted for. It was noticeable that no African delegateshad remained in or near the Hall. They obviously believed more strongly than people from other parts of the world that the South Africans were not in the habit of making empty threats.

Also under the rubble and presumed dead were a number of Seychellois hotel and cleaning staff who had been allowed to enter the Hall to start clearing up. Nobody thought to tell them of the threat and give them the choice to go or stay. Had Hoareau's instructions to evacuate the area been carried out they would also would not have been in the Hall. In all around 20 people were thought to have been caught by the explosion.

Chapter Seventeen

PARADISE LOST

There was nothing more we could do to help so we returned to the Minister's room. We were all booked to leave on a special flight to Hong Kong that evening. Because John Kershaw was still missing in the rubble of the hall, it was decided that someone should remain in Seychelles to assist him if he was found to be alive and to handle the formalities and return the body to New Zealand if he was found to be dead. Nobody volunteered so as the most junior member of the delegation, I was told to remain.

I returned to the wrecked hall to watch progress and see if I could help. One of the local cleaning staff had been found alive but very badly injured. Nobody who was in the hall had been expected to survive the explosion but now that one person had been found alive, efforts took on a greater urgency. Everybody that was physically able to help was being drafted in and I joined a chain that was passing rubble away from the area once it was carefully lifted by one of the police team.

Five dead bodies of Seychellois staff were located during the next half-hour and rescue efforts were beginning to flag when the discovery of a second person alive, the Malaysian delegate, renewed the searchers' hopes. The Malaysian and Singaporean were found together. The latter's body had clearly taken the main force of the blast and provided a degree of protection for the other. The group of five delegates from India, Fiji, Mauritius and Sri Lanka were also found together a little later but none of them had been so fortunate.

They had clearly been very near the centre of the blast and their bodies were horribly mutilated. There was an interruption to the rescue efforts when Hoareau returned. It was an interruption that did nothing to lighten the air of despondency that had settled over the operation. Hoareau grabbed his deputy and demanded to know why he had not cleared the areas as he had been instructed to do. The deputy had responded that Llewellyn had overruled him and said it was not necessary. Hoareau, clearly furious, had scrambled across the rubble to where Llewellyn was working in one of the rescue teams. He had grabbed Llewellyn, who had studiously ignored his approach, and demanded to know why he had overruled the decision to clear the hall. Llewellyn had replied that he was only an advisor and the decision had been taken by Hoareau's man. He had added that it was not his fault if that man found the advice an experienced white-man more compelling than Hoareau's. Hoareau had replied that Llewellyn was not an advisor's arse-hole, he was an idiot and a bloody murderer and he had then knocked Llewellyn down. Llewellyn had risen with a piece of wood in his hand. Both he and Hoareau had been quickly restrained by others.

"I want him out of this place and out of this country today," shouted Hoareau, pointing at Llewellyn. The latter started to argue and then became aware of the lack of sympathy, and indeed of the open hostility on the faces of most of the people around him. He was probably also conscious that he had forfeited the support of his own Minister earlier in the day and would get no-one else's support. He dropped the piece of wood, shook himself loose, and clambered away over the rubble with as much dignity as he could muster in the circumstances.

I took a break from the rescue operations to say farewell to the rest of the New Zealand delegation. The Canadian delegation was leaving on the same plane. I had had in my mind to sit with Simone on the plane. The eight-hour flight to Hong Kong would have given us ample time to discuss whether we wanted to see each other again or simply treat our relationship as an away-from-home fling. That plan had been ruined by my enforced stay in Seychelles and I had been so overwhelmed by events over the last few hours that the thought that Simone would soon be leaving had slipped my mind. Then suddenly she had been before me and we were both at a loss for words. We formally shook hands, said how nice it had been to meet and we must keep in touch. Her eyes told me a lot more than the stilted conversation however. She handed me a handwritten card with her home address in Ottawa and her phone number on it and whispered "please write". I had wanted to hug her and kiss her but there were a lot of other people around and the rest of her delegation were already moving towards the bus. The moment when it would have been possible to kiss her passed and I had been too slow; the story of my life. Simone said goodbye and got on the bus. I will write to her on the plane on the way back to New Zealand I told myself. There will be plenty of time and I often think quite lucidly when I am 35,000 feet in the air, in the comfort of the business class compartment of an airliner and free of most of the distractions f daily life. What was more, I did write to her when I was on the plane on my way home.

Brian Franklyn had given me a pat on the back and said "don't make a holiday out of this now, get back to New Zealand as soon as you can" and then he too had gone. Trevor Barnes nodded and said goodbye and Graham Sharp had shook my hand and told me to take care of myself, try to avoid being shot at again and to do whatever I could for John Kershaw. He had said that if I needed any assistance on that from New Zealand to get straight in touch with him. He left hurriedly as he seemed in danger of becoming emotional, a side of him that I had never seen before. I knew that Kershaw had been one of his proteges and perhaps the relationship had been closer than I had realised. I had not thought anyone could have been fond of Kershaw. ·

I had no desire to stay in Seychelles any longer and would dearly have loved to have left on that bus with the rest of them. But the bus had pulled out and I was still stuck there. I returned to the scene of the rescue operations and had joined the chain gang removing rubble again. The last three missing people to be found were the three of the drafting group, Andrew Mayhew of the British delegation,. Raji Patel from the-Commonwealth Secretariat and John Kershaw. They were found together - all were dead. I formally identified what was left of Kershaw's body and wearily headed for bed. The rest of the arrangements I decided could wait until the next day. I had no idea how one arranged to fly a body from Seychelles to New Zealand. I hoped there was someone in Seychelles who did.

There had been no second bomb. Hoareau's men had finally picked up the Grayling's that evening as they tried to catch a flight out of Seychelles. Sonia Grayling had admitted under questioning that the second bomb had been a bluff which they had introduced in case the bomb that was in the hall had been found.

The last thing I heard before trying to sleep that night was the BBC world news. The South African Prime Minister had made a press statement admitting responsibility for the blast and talking in terms of the retribution they had taken and would continue to take against the enemies of South Africa wherever and whomever they be. I had been right in my view of their motivation. That realisation brought no satisfaction. It also reminded me of their threat to me. Was that like the first bomb, the real thing, or like the second bomb, a bluff?

The following morning I had a call from the reception desk saying there was a person called Virginia at the desk. She had asked for Andrew Mayhew and when they told her that he was unavailable, she had asked for me. I went down to the lobby. Virginia was standing by the desk looking even more beautiful than I remembered. Her beauty and her look of anxiety made my heart leap and fall at the same time. What could I say to her, I thought?

"Peter, Andrew said he would come and see me last night and he didn't come. I phoned the hotel last night but the operator said no outside calls were being taken," she said. "This morning I have heard that there was an explosion at the Conference yesterday and I've rushed straight over, but they just keep saying Andrew must have gone home when the other delegates left yesterday. But he wouldn't have gone without talking to me first, I'm sure of it. Tell me what has happened."

She had grabbed my shoulders as she spoke and the tears were only just being held back.

"I'll tell you," I said, "but come out into the garden where it's quieter" - and more private, I thought. I had never before been placed in the situation of conveying such bad personal news and I needed some time to collect my thoughts. We walked out into the garden and sat on a seat. I was not sure how to start. I could think of no way to break the news gently so I told her quietly that the story she had heard was correct, there had been an explosion just after the Conference had finished and that a number of people who had remained in the hall had been killed. Andrew Mayhew had, unfortunately, been one of them. I could see that the pain was deep but she did not scream or cry out. She wept quietly, and shook her head over and over again, whispering no, no, to herself.

"As soon as I heard about the explosion, I knew that was why he· had not called me last night but I prayed and hoped that I was mistaken," she whispered. "Why did it have to be Andrew?" she looked at me and asked. It was a question that had no answer. "He loved you Virginia," I said. "He told me he was going to ask you to marry him".

The first statement was true. The second an assumption on my part. Mayhew had not actually said he was going to ask her to marry him in so many words but it was the logical conclusion to reach on the basis of what he had told me he felt about her. I thought that would give her some comfort but it seemed to make her feel worse. She threw her arms around me and clung to me and whispered over and over again "why?"

I decided to tell her what Andrew had told me when he spoke to me on Sunday night. I repeated that he had said he loved her, that she was the most wonderful person he had ever met and he could not believe that she was interested in him as a person. He had never really been a ladies' man. It wasn't that he was not interested in women but few women had stayed in a relationship with him much beyond two or three dates. They seemed to find him dull and he seldom knew what to do or say to avoid the inevitable parting. But somehow with Virginia he had found it easy to talk and she seemed to find what he said, mainly about the things he had done in the past and hoped to do in the future, interesting. Andrew had also thought it sentimental nonsense when someone said that two people were made for each other but he had changed his mind because that was how he felt about Virginia and himself. Virginia was leaning on my shoulder, listening carefully to me. Every now and then a sob escaped her but she had stopped crying. She said nothing so I continued talking quietly. I told her that Mayhew had been deeply touched by the gift of her grandfather's briefcase, it had seemed to him such a personal thing for her to do.

As I said this, Virginia burst into tears again. She looked at me sadly and said, "Peter, I feel so dreadful. I lied to Andrew about the briefcase. It was not my grandfather's briefcase at all. It was Andrew's grandfather's briefcase. I was asked to give it to him by someone who had known Andrew's grandfather."

It struck me as somewhat curious but I did not want to alarm her in her present emotional state. So I asked her quietly if she could tell me what had happened. She said she had been telephoned at home about a week ago by a person who said he had known Andrew Mayhew s grandfather very well when he lived in Seychelles. He had something of Richard Mayhew's, that he would like her to give to Andrew. He had come to the house and given her an old but very elaborate briefcase. He had said that Richard Mayhew had asked him just before he died to pass the briefcase on to someone in his family as it had been a gift to him from the woman he loved and it had great sentimental value for him and he wished it to remain in the family. He had written to the family when Richard Mayhew died but they had written back saying they wanted to have nothing to do with Richard Mayhew or any possessuions he had gained from his mistress. Andrew Mayhew was the only other member of the family to have visited Seychelles. He obviously had some traits of his grandfather in him as like Richard Mayhew he had fallen for the charms of a Seychellois woman. He was sure the spirit of Richard Mayhew would be content to know that the briegcase was in Andrew's possession. But Andrew my adopt the family position and refuse to accept it if he knew it was his grandfather's. So it would be best if Virginia told him for now that it had been her grandfather's, was of great sentimental value to her and she wanted Andrew to have it and use it constantly as a reminder of her whenever they were apart. He said she could some time in the future tell him the truth. But for now, a little white lie may be better than the truth,

So she had done what he had suggested. She had been surprised at the strength of Andrew Mayhew's response. He had regarded it as significant on her part to give him something special of her grandfather's. She had been too scared to tell him the truth and had continued with the little white-lie.

I tried to calm her and tell her that no harm had been done but she did not stop admonishing herself. I suggested I drive her back to Victoria. We had little to say to each other during the drive. She was lost in her recriminations and I could think of nothing more I could say that would ease her mind. When I left her at the door of her house I repeated that she should think of the happiness she had given Mayhew and not dwell on her lie about the briefcase. That was not important.

I was wrong. I found out the following day that the lie had been important. I had to spend another week in Seychelles while formalities were sorted out about John Kershaw. In the end, with the permission .of his family he was cremated and I returned to New Zealand with his ashes and handed them over to his parents. During that week I spent a lot of time with Hoareau. Both of us felt in the need of someone to talk to. Hoareau told me in one of these sessions that Sonia Grayling had admitted under questioning how the bomb had been put into the hall, or to be more accurate, how it had been carried in and out of the hall for each session. The carrier had been Andrew Mayhew, and his briefcase had been the bomb. At the last session, Llewellyn had not considered it necessary to search the British delegation more than cursorily. It had not been the South Africans' intention to blow up the hall.

They had had a bug placed in the room of the British Minister throughout the Conference. As a consequence, they had felt confident up until the last session.that Britain would stand firm against sanctions. They had been amazed and angered to hear when the Minister returned to his room with his staff after the final session that Britain had changed its position and a resolution in favour of sanctions had been carried. They had been infuriated by what they saw as the British betrayal, though she added that their history should have taught them never to trust the British. They had intended to exact their revenge on the British. They thought that Mayhew would have left the hall along with the others and that he would have been in the Minister's room with the rest of the British delegation. When they had detonated the bomb they had been surprised to see that it was the Conference Hall and not the British delegation's hotel room that had been blown up.

She had refused to be drawn on whether or not Mayhew had been a willing accomplice or an unwitting one. "Work it out for yourselves" she had repeated whenever they pressed her. Hoareau had said that he could not see how Mayhew could have been duped into being the bomb carrier. As far as he was concerned Mayhew must have been part of the team. He recalled that Mayhew had tried to persuade Sir Robin Hollarn to change his mind about supporting sanctions at the lunch time meeting in Baptiste' s suite. I argued that if Mayhew was a collaborator he would not have blown himself up. Hoareau had responded that Mayhew had been the carrier of the bomb but it was not his finger that had been on the trigger. Mayhew had obviously let his 'masters' down and so had been eliminated.

I said nothing more at the time. I agonised over the choice that night. If I said nothing, Mayhew's reputation would carry the stigma forever. If I explained how the briefcase had come into Mayhew's possession, Virginia would face suspicion and interrogation. That would be a most unpleasant experience at any time and doubly unpleasant in her present emotional state. But even worse, I had an uneasy feeling that the revelation that she had in effect been responsible for Mayhew's death could destroy her. He was dead- did his reputation matter?. She was alive and could do without the burden of his death on her conscience. I was still undecided what to do when I fell into the sleep of the utterly exhausted that night.

Milton Keynes UK
Ingram Content Group UK Ltd.
UKHW040414251123
433027UK00009BB/180/J

9 781669 881032